I0768870

The Royal Gambit

A Vexia Novella

Mallory Wanless

Cover design by GetCovers

First edition

ISBN:

Paperback: 979-8-9888284-4-0

Ebook: 979-8-9888284-3-3

ONE

In the weeks following her husband's passing—assassination—Queen Irena struggled to maintain control of the royal court. It didn't help that she would get winded walking across a room—damn this exhausting pregnancy. Still, the royal guards had never taken orders from a woman and apparently, didn't feel comfortable following her *very* clear directions.

She'd repeat herself a dozen times before someone finally did as she ordered. Irena didn't think she was being unreasonable. Her commands were never outside the scope of their original job descriptions, but damn those sexist guards. They'd continuously look to her advisor before following her instructions. Gustave was her oldest advisor and a bit old-fashioned. He deferred to her publicly, but when they were with her council, that old man was quick to point out all the reasons her plans wouldn't work, but rarely followed up with advice on how to improve things.

Since she had been married to the king at the time of his

demise, and was still carrying his unborn child, she had the authority to assume power in the kingdom. At least until the child was born. If it were a boy, she'd be granted the title of Queen Mother and rule until he came of age. If the child happened to be a girl, she'd be forced to remarry quickly if she wanted to keep her crown. And that was only *if* she truly decided she wanted to be queen permanently. Well, a figurehead queen. Unless she found a malleable man to rule publicly while she directed his decisions behind the scenes. Then he could be her puppet and she could really get shit done.

Rubbing her swollen belly thoughtfully, Irena wondered what it would be like to be married to a man who respected her, listened to her, *loved* her. She'd never had a man like that before. She couldn't even imagine it.

Hells, she didn't need a man. She could rule on her own.

Irena was excited at the prospect of being able to make real, *lasting* change in Ravendale. Hells, in the whole country of Mistfall. But she'd start small. Improving the lives of those within the city walls. Her first project was to improve the children's home she'd been working and living in just before she married the king.

After King Odker had killed his third bride and the other kingdoms and families of rank refused to send him any more of their daughters, he'd decided to seek out a child bride. That's when he'd drunkenly stumbled into the children's home and Irena had put herself in his path. It was her job to protect the children and she didn't regret a single action she'd taken to catch his eye and become his wife. They were married within a week and he raped her nightly until she conceived their first child. By her second trimester, she knew she had to do something to rid herself, and the world, of that vile man.

As a child, Irena had grown up first on the streets of Ravendale and later in the very home she'd been working in when Odker found her. Leah and Tameer had taken her under their wing, teaching her how to pick pockets and defend herself. Unfortunately, the leader of their little guild was a violent asshole. At only twelve, Shithead had been the oldest kid in their off-shoot of the Thieves Guild and had decided that that made him the leader. He collected a "tax" from each child at the start of every day, claiming some of what they'd stolen the night before. If you didn't have enough to pay his tax, he'd take it out on your flesh.

Irena still vividly recalled that horrible night when Shithead had come to collect her tax. She'd been only eight and hadn't stolen enough coin to pay him, so she'd spent the day hiding out, hoping to avoid his notice. She'd never been that lucky, but she prayed to the Mother that just this once, she'd be safe.

She might as well have prayed for a loving family to come through town and adopt her, taking her back to their mansion to live a happy, healthy, safe life.

Shithead found her cowering under the bridge just as the sun was setting. Decades later, the memory of that night still haunted Irena's nightmares. If Leah hadn't found her and killed that bastard, Irena was sure she would never have seen another sunrise.

Shaking her head, Irena refocused on the problems in front

of her. The children's home needed to be rebuilt from the ground up, if she was being completely honest, but Irena didn't think she could convince her advisors to go for that. Instead, she'd settle for an installation of indoor plumbing—they had the technology in the richer neighborhoods, it would be easy enough to extend it to the lower-income areas. And insulating the entire building. Irena could clearly remember the sound of the wind whistling through the cracks in the walls of the clapboard building.

If she could also convince her advisors to pry open their purse strings more, she'd like to supply the house with new beds and fresh clothing for all the children. However, she was already in talks with the farmers outside of Ravendale's walls to donate their excess hay to refill the children's mattresses. It wouldn't be the best, but it would be better than the moldy, lumpy beds the children slept on now.

"Your Majesty?" The voice of her handmaiden drew Irena out of her plans. By the sound of the woman's voice, she'd likely been trying to get Irena's attention for a while.

"Yes? Sorry, Nicolette. My mind was elsewhere. What did you need?" Irena rubbed her belly absentmindedly, feeling the bulge of an elbow or a knee driving her taut skin to an odd shape.

"You have a guest waiting in the throne room." The woman never once lifted her gaze to meet Irena's. Despite Irena's best efforts, the staff still wouldn't look her in the eye.

"A guest?" she inquired while slowly pushing up from her chair to follow the woman to the throne room.

"Yes, Your Majesty. He said he was your brother." The last word lifted at the end; almost a question but not quite. None of the staff dared question her. When King Odker had reigned, questions were met with swift and brutal violence. Gods, Irena really hated that man and the torment he wrought on these poor people.

Irena froze mid-step, her mind catching up to what her handmaiden had just said.

Her brother?

Two

"Tam! Oh my gods! What are you doing here?" Irena ran up to her adopted brother and dear friend as quickly as her swollen ankles would allow and wrapped her arms tightly around his neck. After weeks of being surrounded by staff who were actively avoiding her and advisors who were constantly undermining her and questioning her decisions, it was a relief to see a friendly face.

Tameer's arms wrapped around her, lifting her up as he twirled them before setting her firmly back on the ground. "Hello, darling. I'm sorry I didn't send word before showing up here. I had to get out of that house." He shuddered as if he'd seen something ghastly. "The noises. Gods, the noises."

Irena clutched his hands. "Is everything ok? Leah? What happened?"

Tameer shook his head. "She's gone and gotten herself... entangled." The exasperated sigh that followed conveyed more than words could. In Tameer's eyes, to be entangled in love was tantamount to signing one's own death warrant.

Irena laughed and swatted his arm. "Tam, you had me worried! I thought something was *actually* wrong."

"Something *is* wrong," he protested. "She spends all of her free time with that ex-captain of *your* guard, fucking like rabbits and making the most grotesque and pornographic sounds you could possibly imagine."

Irena cackled at the look of utter disgust on Tameer's face. "Well, whatever the reason, I'm glad you're here. I could use someone I can trust to help me navigate this shit."

"What's going on, kiddo?" Tam took her hand and tucked it into the crook of his arm, guiding her down the hall and out into the famous rose gardens.

Irena loved this spot. With the roses in bloom, it was filled with the most peaceful and intoxicating scent. She spent all her free time—which wasn't much, unfortunately—soaking up the sun and basking in the sweet perfume of the roses in this magical place.

Tameer led her to a bench under the crepe myrtles and took a seat beside her, never letting go of her hand. "Talk to me."

Irena inhaled deeply, taking courage and comfort in the floral fragrance that surrounded them. "I can't seem to get my advisors to actually listen to me," she admitted on an exhale. It was embarrassing to vocalize her issues, but the fucking *men* in her council were hells-bent on questioning her at every turn and it was utterly draining. "I just want to improve the lives of the people here, especially the children and those in dangerous or violent situations that need help getting out. I want to take care of our people, dammit! Why do they keep treating me like a naive child? I'm their godsdamn queen. Doesn't that mean anything?" Irena stood up and began pacing, finally unleashing all the frustration and rage she'd been bottling up in an effort to portray a level-headed, agreeable royal. "I proposed increasing the tax on the lords of the merchant district by one percent. *One percent*, Tam! And do you know what they said to me? 'We can't tax the rich. We need them to keep the economy moving. Taxing them will drive them away.' Are you fucking kidding me?!" She was fuming now. The more she thought about it, the more she wanted to punch those arrogant, old, assholes in their wrinkly pale faces.

Suddenly, Tam was filling her field of vision. Irena had to stop short or she'd trample him. He caught her arms before she fell back in her attempts to avoid running him over. "Whoa, there." Tam chuckled as he righted her. "It sounds like a shit show here. Are you sure you even want to be here? You know Leah and I would *love* it if you and the baby came to stay with us. Hells, you can come with me right now. You being there would definitely put a stop to all of their obnoxious shenanigans."

Irena scoffed. "Are you saying I'm so disgustingly fat that my mere presence in a home would kill anyone else's libido?"

"What? No! I definitely didn't mean it like that." Tam tried to recover as a violent flush brightened his face. "I just meant, with you being all royal... and pregnant... you're like a walking reminder that sex leads to more humans. I don't know about Ash, but I know Leah isn't interested in having a baby any time soon."

Irena laughed. It wasn't easy to fluster Tameer, but damn it was fun when she did. "I'm just picking on you." She grinned up at him, watching the redness fade from his face. "I appreciate the offer, but I really think I can do good here. It's an uphill fight to get the council to agree to anything, but I'm far too stubborn to back down now."

Warmth glowed in Tameer's eyes as he nodded. "You definitely do have that stubborn defiance that royals seem to have in spades. So how can I help? What do you need?"

"According to the council? I need a husband."

A mischievous smile pulled at Tameer's lips. "I think I know just the guy."

"Tam, an engagement to a criminal isn't going to legitimize my reign."

"No, that's the best part! He's not a criminal. He's a prince! Second son of the King of Westera. He's hiding out in Vexia because his mom has been trying to marry him off for months."

Irena pressed her fingers to her temples, trying to massage away the headache that was already starting. She hadn't even had her morning tea yet. Gods, did she even want to rule this damn country? As if in answer to her question, the baby swimming around in her belly elbowed her bladder. Right. Whether she wanted to be queen or not, she had an obligation to her people to make right the wrongs of her thankfully dead husband and try to improve their country for her child and all the other children in Mistfall.

She gently rubbed her belly and refocused her attention on her beloved friend. "Tam, be serious. Do you really think I should marry some arrogant, entitled man-child? Not to mention, his mother sounds outrageously controlling and I really don't need to add another abusive adult to this little love's life. We just got their father out of the way. I'm not about to add a crazed step-grandma to my family tree."

"I'm not saying you have to actually marry him." Tameer smiled conspiratorially. "Just tell the country you're betrothed. It will get your advisors off your back, legitimize your rule, and you don't even have to go through with it! Especially if my little nibling turns out to be a nephew." His smile warmed as his focus shifted to her belly. Tameer raised his hand, letting it hover just over her belly, a question in his gaze. When she nodded, he immediately lowered his hand to rest on her swollen stomach. Her baby kicked Tameer's hand instantly. She and Tameer both laughed at the connection her adopted brother already had with her unborn child.

Sighing heavily, she placed her hand over his. "I just don't know about this. I don't love the idea of lying to the people. King Odker was a lying, cheating, monster of a man. I don't want to do anything that might put me in the same category as him. Our people deserve better."

Tam released his hold on her belly and placed both hands on either side of her neck, his thumbs gently rubbing along her cheeks, wiping away tears she hadn't realized she'd been crying. "Irena, you are *nothing* like that son of a bitch. You are a godsdamned angel and Mistfall is lucky to have you." His eyes locked on hers, holding her steady and reinforcing his words. "You are a badass, brilliant, compassionate person and the people of Mistfall will figure that out, sooner rather than later. You aren't lying to them. You are doing what you need to in order to ensure that they have the best possible queen reigning over them. It's not your fault the royal council is full of misogynistic asshats."

Irena laughed despite herself, leaning into Tameer and resting her head on his chest. The steady thump of his heart under her cheek and the warmth of his body were so calming. "Can you just stay here forever? Can I marry you instead?"

Tameer chuckled, rubbing his hand up and down the length of her spine. "Darling, as much as I would love to be here with you every day, playing with that sweet baby and watching you fix this fucking place, you really aren't my type. Unless you've grown a dick since we were kids...?" He pulled back and eyed her in mock suspicion, eyebrow raised incredulously.

Irena winked dramatically, causing Tameer to snort with laughter. He pulled her back into a tight embrace. "Regardless," he continued, "I doubt your council would approve of your engagement to the former leader of the Thieves Guild. I don't think that would give you the credibility you need to keep your fancy-ass crown."

Groaning in defeat, Irena nodded into Tameer's solid chest. "Fine, bring me your prince. I'm not promising to marry him.

Or pretend to marry him. But I'll meet him."

Tameer placed a soft kiss on her forehead. "You won't regret it."

Irena really hoped he was right.

THREE

Dimitri groaned as he rolled over and slowly pressed himself up and out of bed. The overwhelming fragrance of the wisteria blooms curtaining the headboard made his stomach roil.

Although, to be fair to the purple blossoms, that could have also been a result of the copious amounts of whisky he'd indulged in the night before. Whisky. It was nothing like the delicious flavor of the spiced ouzo from back home, but damn if it didn't do the trick just as well. Drowning out the voices of his family constantly telling him all the ways he was failing them—and Westera at large—was a job for only the strongest of liquors.

Dimitri knew they meant well, but he couldn't take another person telling him how he wasn't living up to expectations. It was his job as the second son to marry wealth or royalty to strengthen their kingdom. At twenty-five he should have been married with a second child on the way by now. Instead, he was hiding out in a backwater town in another country to escape their critiques.

It wasn't that Dimitri didn't want to get married, someday, but he was young. He wanted to enjoy his freedom before he was shackled to some spoiled princess or wannabe princess. He sure as hells didn't want to be a father yet. Hells, he had no idea how to take care of someone else. He was barely taking care of himself these days.

Thus, the intense pounding in his head and seemingly endless bouts of nausea courtesy of one too many bottles last night.

He must have drifted back to sleep because Dimitri woke to the sun directly in his eyes and the overly chipper innkeeper knocking a little too loudly on his door.

"Enter," he groaned. Gods, was that his voice? It sounded raw and distant. Maybe bottles of straight whisky weren't good for one's throat.

"Good afternoon, sir." The innkeeper used her hip to push up the door, carrying a tray of what appeared to be dry toast and black coffee. "I brought you some refreshments. Tameer warned me that you might need something bland and simple after your night out, so I've brought the simplest of sustenance and the blackest coffee." She placed the tray on the table under the open window and turned to face him. "If you feel the need to expel your stomach contents, there's a chamberpot under your bed. We have indoor plumbing, of course, but only in the communal washroom at the end of the hall. I would request that you not vomit out the window, as there are vendors selling their wares in the market below you."

Damn. He'd never met such a blunt, matter-of-fact woman in his life. Dimitri was used to being catered to. Literally everyone in his life—with the exception of his parents and his older brother—was beneath him and spoke to him accordingly. This woman. This tiny little small-town innkeeper spoke to him like he was just another drunk sleeping it off at her overly floral inn. Which, he realized, he was. Dimitri had made a point to look as un-princely as possible, concealing his identity in self-preservation as much as to avoid his parents finding him until he was truly ready.

Wait, Tameer? She said Tameer told her what he'd need this morning. Dimitri didn't know anyone in this godsforsaken town. So why did that name sound familiar?

"If you need anything else, just pull the chain by the bedside. It will ring a bell by the front desk and I'll be right up." Her smile was friendly and open. Not at all the forced, showy smiles he got back home. This one was genuine. It was so strange to be treated with such openness and kindness. Dimitri almost felt bad for lying to the woman about his true identity. Not bad enough to reveal his parentage, but enough to return her smile with one of his own before mumbling a quiet "thanks" as she slipped out of the room, gently closing the door behind her.

Dimitri slowly shifted himself out of the bed and—with deliberate and careful steps—crossed the small room and sat in the hard wooden chair at the bistro table beside the room's open window. From here, the smell of the wisteria was considerably lighter and actually quite nice. He picked up the mug of coffee, inhaling the scent of the precious liquid before taking a long, slow sip and awakening his senses. The plain toast was exactly what he needed to absorb the last of the alcohol rolling around in his stomach. By the time he'd finished off the tray, he almost felt human again.

Now, to find that communal washroom she mentioned.

Caffeinated and relatively clean, Dimitri nearly felt like himself once more. He still hadn't dared ingest anything more than the innkeeper's dry toast, but he was feeling well enough to venture out of the inn and explore the town he'd chosen to be his hideout. Before exiting the inn, he'd inquired after the man she'd mentioned when the innkeeper—Maddie, he was fairly certain—had woken him.

His name was Tameer, she reminded him. Apparently, he lived with the baker on the other side of their small town. Dimitri, having nothing better to do with his time, decided to find the man and see just how much he'd revealed in his drunken state.

The town itself was rather picturesque if one ignored the sheer number of weapons the townsfolk kept on their person, seemingly at all times. The small cottages were mostly made of stone, with solid wood doors and curtained windows. Much to Dimitri's surprise, it seemed that very few people locked their doors. In a town known for its high percentage of criminal elements, it was a bit shocking to see no one locking up as they left their homes. Hells, a few didn't even bother to close their doors.

Dimitri passively wondered if there was something to that "honor among thieves" motto he'd heard from time to time.

The open-air market outside the inn was filled with merchants hawking all conceivable wares. From weapons and armor to charms and supposed love spells, this town seemed to have everything.

Maddie told him that Tameer lived with the town's baker and would likely be found selling off her excess breads and baked goods at the market. If not there, she'd given him directions to their home. Another odd thing about the town. Dimitri couldn't imagine anyone giving a stranger—a foreigner, no less—directions to someone's home in Sypris. Either this town was full of very naive individuals, or they knew someone committing a crime in this criminal town wouldn't last long. Dimitri thought it was likely the latter. Only a fool steals from master thieves.

Dimitri strolled casually down the gravel road, browsing the stands while keeping an eye out for the baker's stall. He smelled the baker's table before he saw it. Scents of warm, buttery bread, sweet cakes, and cinnamon called to him, drawing him in like a siren's call.

A man stood behind the table, straightening up a platter of cookies. He wasn't what Dimitri had been expecting, although to be fair, he hadn't known what to expect. This man was built like a damn warrior. Broad shoulders, thick arms, calloused hands, and well-maintained hair.

"Hello there. Are you, by chance, Tameer?" Dimitri asked cautiously. This was not a man to be trifled with and if Dimitri had shared too much while he was in his cups, he didn't think he could pay this man off. He sure as hells couldn't stop him physically.

The man turned to face Dimitri, a single eyebrow disappearing behind the hair hanging over his forehead. "Who wants to know?" His voice was gruff and demanding.

"Apologies," Dimitri said quickly. "My name is—" Gods, what name would he have given last night? "Ah, my name is…" Dimitri trailed off, completely at a loss.

"Son, if you don't know your own name, you really shouldn't be wandering around with this lot. They have a code of ethics, mind you, but you make yourself a walking target roaming without name or weapon to defend yourself." The giant's eyes roved over him, a hint of concern in his face before he quickly quashed it. "Regardless, I'm not the man you want. He's gone."

"Oh, gone?" That's disconcerting. Where could he have gone and why would he have rushed off so quickly after spending a night drinking it up with a prince in hiding? Dimitri couldn't help but worry as his mind immediately flew to the worst possible scenarios.

"Aye, he had business in the capital."

Shit shit shit. Not only had that man learned his identity, but he'd rushed off to tell the local authorities and likely use this knowledge to his benefit somehow. No doubt, Dimitri's mother would pay handsomely for his safe return. She had a myriad of rich potential wives lined up for him back home.

Taking a few calming breaths, Dimitri tossed a few coppers on the counter, grabbed what appeared to be a blueberry scone, and thanked the man before heading back to the inn as nonchalantly as possible.

He needed to find this Tameer before things truly got out of control.

Four

Dimitri debated how best to approach Tameer, once he finally found him, and settled on simply being direct. Hells, this man lived in a town of criminals and those known to be hiding from one thing or another. Chances were good that Tameer would have his own demons from which he was hiding. Dimitri hoped Tameer would be sympathetic to his cause. Or at least open to a bribe to give Dimitri a head start before reporting his location to his mother. In his experience, everyone had a price, it was just a matter of finding it.

He'd initially planned to head straight for the capital and try to catch Tameer before he reached the king or queen of this land, but decided against it. Dimitri had spent half the day in bed and didn't even learn about Tameer's potential knowledge of him until the man had already left town. There was no way Dimitri could stop him from whatever business he had in the capital. He just hoped he wasn't on the list of things Tameer was handling in court.

Irena was not thrilled by the fake betrothal plan, but after that meeting with her "advisors"—if she could even call them that—she started to wonder if it truly was the best course of action. Her advisors were more like a collection of old men who kept telling her all the reasons why her ideas were stupid, pointless, and naive. Irena wasn't a violent woman, but she really wanted to slap each and every one of them in their smug faces.

"You could just fire them, you know." Tameer was lounging in her deep armchair, one ankle resting on his knee and a book in his lap.

Irena collapsed heavily in the chair across from him. Leaning her head back against the soft fabric, she rubbed her belly and exhaled slowly. "I can't. Not yet anyway. The king just died. If I throw out his entire cabinet as well, it will look suspicious. Like I was behind his death and organized a minor coup."

"Well, that is kind of what happened," Tameer smirked.

"Yes, but I'm not a suspect right now and I'd like to keep it that way. Not to mention, I'm not even sure I have that kind of authority." She glared at him through half-lidded eyes. Gods, she was just so damn tired. She desperately wished to have people in her employ that she could genuinely trust. People she could rely on to handle the small things so she could actually rest. Maybe even take a nap. Pregnancy was so much harder than she'd ever imagined and all she wanted to do was get out of that godsdamned corset and into her bed.

Instead, she forced herself to sit upright and focus on Tameer. "What have you learned about this prince of yours?"

"I've consulted with a few… we'll call them friends, but I'm using the term *very* loosely. He's the second son of a mercantile kingdom. His father passed a few years ago and his brother has been ruling ever since. Decent guy, by all accounts, if a bit of a stickler to the laws. Married a princess from a neighboring country. Couple of rug rats. His mother, Queen Mother Sophia, isn't exactly 'bad' but she seems to be very set in her ways. She doesn't like that her twenty-something son is unmarried and by all accounts a fun-loving slacker."

"And you think *he'd* make a smart match for me? I'm going to have a baby soon, I don't need to take care of a man-child as well."

Tameer chuckled but nodded. "Point taken, but I think he could give your claim to the throne the legitimacy you need and get your advisors off your back."

Irena sighed, sitting back in her chair and putting her feet up on the coffee table between them. It was unladylike behavior, but her ankles were so swollen that her feet had begun to puff up around the straps of her slippers. She really needed a damn break. "Fine. I don't like this plan, but I suppose it can't possibly make things worse. Hells, maybe he'll even be helpful. That would be fucking amazing."

Closing her eyes for a moment, Irena allowed herself a brief respite to imagine what it could be like to rule with a true partner. Someone who could help make the hard choices and support her endeavors to improve Mistfall.

She hadn't meant to fall asleep, but when she opened her eyes again, Tameer was nearly halfway through the book he'd been reading and the sun was sinking behind the walls, painting the sky a beautiful magenta.

Groaning, she sat up and rubbed the sleep from her eyes.

"Ah, good! You're up. I just got word back from Leah. She'll find the prince and make sure my intel is accurate before we bother trying to bring him here."

Irena blinked. Her brain couldn't process what her brother just said. "Come again?"

Tameer leaned forward, placing his book on the table, and poured her a steaming cup of floral-scented tea. He added a couple of iced cookies on the saucer beside the cup and rose to bring them to her. Setting the cup and saucer on the arm of her chair, Tameer took a seat on the table. Looking pointedly at the tea and cookies, Tameer waited for her to sit up and take a bite before he spoke.

Rolling her eyes, Irena took a single bite from the cinnamon-iced cookie and gestured for him to get on with it.

Still, that stubborn ass of a man waited for her to chew, swallow, and take a second bite before he spoke. "While you were busy this morning, I sent a raven to Leah with the briefest of messages as well as a description of the prince. An hour ago, while Your Highness was taking her royal—and might I add, rather uncomfortable looking—nap, I got a missive back. Apparently, the prince came by the market stand looking for me." He raised a meaningful eyebrow, implying that the prince seeking him out was something noteworthy. Either because she was exhausted or perhaps it was the "pregnancy fog" her handmaidens sometimes spoke of, but Irena didn't understand the significance of the prince looking for Tameer. Hadn't they spent the night drinking? Perhaps the man was just looking for another night of revelry.

When it was clear she wasn't catching on, Tameer rolled his eyes and continued. "He must know that I know who he is. He's hiding from his mother, as we know thanks to my informants. Perhaps he's worried I'll rat him out." Tameer paused, rubbing his chin thoughtfully. "I guess I kind of did, but not in a really bad way, right? I mean, I told you, but *only* you, and it's not like you're going to deport him or anything."

"No, I'm just going to trap him in a sham marriage to be a stepfather to my dead abuser's child." Irena didn't harbor any resentment toward the baby for how they'd been created, but she knew not everyone would feel that way. The chances of this prince agreeing to marry her while she's fighting to keep her kingdom and carrying another man's child? It was unlikely at best.

Tameer *tsk*ed. "It wouldn't be a sham marriage. A sham engagement, perhaps, but you don't have to follow through with the wedding. Just keep him around until the baby is born. If you have a son, then you no longer need a husband and all this will be moot."

"And if I have a daughter?" Irena pressed.

Tameer grinned, a wicked gleam in his eyes. "Did I mention how very dashing the prince is?"

FIVE

"You there! Hold on. I need to talk to you."

Shit.

Dimitri tried to duck into the crowded market and escape the voice that shouted after him. Perhaps if he could slip into the mass of people, he could lose them and find Tameer before the royal guards inevitably came to pick him up and send him back to his mother's controlling arms.

"Hey! I just need to—ugh." The shouting was cut off but Dimitri didn't chance a look back to see why. He dodged busy shoppers, moving as swiftly and deftly as he could through the throngs of people.

When he felt reasonably confident that he'd lost his pursuer, Dimitri turned down an alleyway and began making his way back toward the inn. He needed to collect his belongings and get the hells out of this town while he still could.

Something sharp pricked the side of his neck, filling him

with an instant wave of nausea as a tingling sensation spread from the sight of the injury.

"Gods, did you have to poison him?" A gruff male voice spoke, but Dimitri couldn't find the source. His vision was quickly fading to black as he lost control of his limbs and slid to the rough stone path.

"He was getting away," a flippant female voice replied. "Now he's not."

"No. Thanks to you, now he's dead weight."

"Good thing you have all those rippling muscles," came the sultry female voice. Dimitri thought there might have been some heat in her words, but he couldn't be sure.

Seconds later, he felt himself get lifted off the ground and thrown over an enormously muscled shoulder. Darkness swallowed him as he was carried away.

Dimitri woke to the overwhelmingly sweet scent of cinnamon and icing. He didn't move just yet, hearing an argument nearby. He tried to focus on their words as he fought to shake the fuzzy feeling from his mind.

"I can't believe you told a complete *stranger* where Tam was. Gods, are you sure you were a guard? That's the idiotic behavior of a naive child."

Damn, she sounded pissed. Her voice was faintly familiar. Dimitri thought she must have been the person yelling at him before he'd been struck by some kind of poison dart.

"I didn't know he was a stranger," came the slightly dejected voice of the man who'd assisted in Dimitri's capture.

"Did you know him?"

"Well, no. But I'm still new here. I don't know everyone like you two."

A loud, exasperated sigh filled the room. "It's a good thing you're cute." Dimitri thought he heard a smile in her voice, the anger quickly fading. "Soldier boy, you can't go around assuming we know everyone. If you don't know them, don't tell them shit, ok? Tam still has enemies in the capital. I haven't had to chase off an attempted assassin in a while, but I'm not going to assume that means they've given up on killing him."

Peeking through his eyelashes, Dimitri saw the mountain of a man pull the pink-haired woman into a warm embrace, placing a kiss on her head as he nodded his agreement.

The man locked eyes with Dimitri. *Shit.* He'd been caught. Releasing his hold on the woman, the man crossed the room and positioned himself right beside Dimitri's head.

Giving up the act, he opened his eyes fully and took in the room around him. He was lying on a vibrant purple couch with a low table before it, covered in plates of sweets, desserts, and a steaming teapot. The room seemed to practically glow with warmth and a sense of home he never even felt at his own home. A little voice in the back of his mind warned Dimitri that it was likely a trick of some kind, but he just couldn't bring himself to care.

The pink-haired woman—a fae, he was almost certain—smiled at him, her eyes twinkling. "Good morning, darling. How did you sleep?"

"It's three in the afternoon, Leah." The grumpy man standing beside the couch sighed with an air of annoyance that Dimitri felt was entirely unwarranted. He was about to say as much when the woman, Leah, *tsk*ed her guard and waved him off.

The man grunted to express his disapproval, but the beautiful fae woman gave him a look that Dimitri couldn't read, although, to be fair, he wasn't trying that hard. The sooner the mountain of a grump left, the sooner Dimitri could turn on the charm and win this woman's favor.

One last look of annoyance and the mountain left them, closing the door behind him as he did.

"Finally," Leah said with a sigh. "I thought he'd never leave!" She crossed the room and climbed onto the couch beside him, turning sideways to face him and tucking her legs beneath her. She looked so small and childlike. Dimitri instantly felt compelled to protect her from any and all threats.

"So tell me, darling. Why are you looking for my friend Tameer?" She reached up and gently tucked a lock of hair behind his ear, her fingers lingering on his jaw for a fraction of a second. When Dimitri moved to lean into her touch, she slipped her hand away. "How do you know him?"

Know who? Dimitri thought. His mind was a muddled haze. The only thing clear was the majestic creature before him and his undeniable urge to tell her anything and everything she wanted to know.

That can't be right. Dimitri was a sucker for a gorgeous

woman, to be sure, but he'd never wanted to spill his secrets to anyone. And yet, as he looked into her lavender eyes, he wanted to tell Leah his entire life story.

He shifted on the couch, pulling one leg under him while leaving the other firmly planted on the floor. Facing her head-on, he could just make out the hints of magic at the periphery of his vision. He'd been trained to spot and break down illusions. His tutors would be disappointed that he hadn't seen this one the instant he awoke. Still, he could play along, for now.

"I don't know him," Dimitri replied. His voice sounded light and distant. *Must be more of her magic at work.*

"Then why did you seek him out?" Her words sounded harder now, his mind cutting through some of her magic. The warm, borderline-glittering gleam of the room began to fade as well.

"I met him at the tavern. He was a good drinking buddy. I was… hoping for another round." Dimitri stumbled over the last few words. Her magic seemed to be making it hard for him to spin a web of lies, so he'd have to settle for half-truths.

Leah seemed to study his face and Dimitri smiled, hoping to disarm her with his charm. He'd wooed many a lass with his dimples and winning smile. A fae girl from a town of criminals shouldn't be too hard.

A hint of something flashed in her eyes, but it was gone a second later. Leah leaned closer, resting her arm along the back of the couch while casually reaching out and twirling his hair around her fingers. A wave of warmth washed over him. Dimitri could feel her magic pulling him under again, he just couldn't bring himself to care, so long as she continued touching him.

Leah moved closer still, shifting her weight until she was practically in his lap, both hands in his hair as she pulled his face closer to hers. Brushing her nose against his lips, his jaw, down to his ear, her smooth voice wrapped around him like a silk blanket. "Why do you really want to find Tameer?"

Her breath was a warm whisper on his neck, sending shivers down his spine as she gently tugged at the hair at the base of his skull. He knew she was compelling him with her magic, but he was helpless to stop her. "I need to know what all he knows about me."

That got her attention. Leah pulled back a moment, eyebrows raised in intrigue. She stood without releasing her hold on his hair, turning him forward and climbing onto him, straddling his thighs with her own. She pulled his hair once more, forcing his head back to look up at her as she wiggled slightly on his lap. "Who are you?" Her tongue teased his earlobe as the words slipped from her talented lips.

Dimitri's mind pushed back, trying to pull away from her skilled, magical interrogation. As though she felt him fighting her, Leah pulled his earlobe into her mouth, biting just hard enough to elicit a groan from him as he tried to keep his lips clamped shut.

"Who. Are. You?" She punctuated each word with a less-than-gentle bite. Earlobe, neck, bottom lip. The temptress of a woman pulled away, her lips hovering just out of reach as he moaned at the electric shock her bites sent through his body.

"My name is..." he grunted, trying to fight the pull of her magic, but ultimately failed. "Dimitri Aetos." He screwed his lips tightly shut, but it was too late. The words were out there.

"Aetos," she sighed into him, pressing her luscious curves into his chest and almost making him forget the dangerous truth he'd just admitted against his will. "That's quite the royal name, don't you think, dearest?"

Dimitri looked up. The angry mountain was glaring down at them. If looks could kill, Dimitri was certain he would have been a pile of useless flesh. Which, all things considered, might not be a terrible way to go.

A growl escaped the man as he ground his teeth, then he rounded the table and lifted Leah from Dimitri's lap as though she weighed nothing. Pinning her between the wall and his massive frame, he captured her lips in an angry and possessive kiss that left Dimitri feeling like an interloper and both his captors breathless.

Dimitri cleared his throat loudly, hoping to remind his kidnappers that he was, in fact, still in the room. Leah chuckled in response while the mountain of a man pinned Dimitri with a rage-filled glare.

Dimitri raised his hands in surrender. "I didn't do anything. She climbed in *my* lap."

The man clenched and unclenched his fists several times before Leah placed both of her hands on his cheeks and pulled his attention back to her. "He's right, love. I was interrogating him. Did you know he's a royal? Second son, I'm guessing. From Westera."

Dimitri balked. How had she figured all of that out simply by his surname? It's not like the use of surnames was commonplace with royals. She must have been well versed in the goings-on of royalty to connect the meager dots he'd given her. Gods, that was terrifying. Dimitri wasn't sure he'd be able to get out of this one unscathed.

"Close your mouth, honey. You look like a dying fish." Leah smirked at him, releasing her guard dog and coming to sit across from him in an overstuffed armchair. "Why are you hiding out in Vexia, young prince? Seems like an odd place for a royal vacation."

Dimitri racked his brain for an answer that was far from the truth, but reasonable enough to get him out of this magicked place. Every time he opened his mouth to respond with a carefully crafted lie, no sound would come out.

"Trouble, darling?" There was a knowing smirk on the fae's face as she watched him struggle. She nodded to the carvings along the door frame and the windows. "Runes. Just the right combination, carved in just the right order, makes it impossible to tell a lie. So, would you like to try again?"

Stunned, Dimitri weighed his options: say nothing and run the risk of being tortured by the aggressive, annoyed-looking man looming over him from the mantle, or tell her just enough of the truth to get the hells out of here.

The truth won out. Well, truth-adjacent. No need to reveal his entire life story to these murderous criminals. "I am the second son of Westera, as you inferred. I'm here to... delay my mother's attempts to marry me off."

The man huffed a laugh, resulting in a chastising look from Leah. "Hush, you. You aren't eager to get hitched either."

A faint color bloomed over the man's face at her words. Dimitri wasn't sure what the situation was between those two, but he really needed to get out of their house before he accidentally revealed more than was absolutely necessary. "I was at the tavern the other night and met your friend Tameer. I'm not sure how much I told to him about my situation and I was hoping to seek him out and request his discretion."

"Why are you hiding?" The man's voice was gruff and edged with distrust.

"I'm not hiding, per se. Just... avoiding unwanted responsibilities."

The man grunted but said nothing more. Leah studied him for several long minutes. Dimitri started to worry that she might be able to read his mind. He wasn't sure exactly how much fae blood she had in her, and therefore didn't know how much magic she had. Some fae were able to manipulate reality. Others could read auras and get inside people's heads. He prayed to the God of Deception that she wasn't that skilled.

After an uncomfortable silence, she nodded, seeming to decide something, and rose from the chair. "Tam's not here right now, but he should be back by the end of the week. He went to see the queen. He didn't say why, but I'm sure it's not about you. Or, at least, not entirely about you."

Shit. "I, uh... all right. Thank you." Dimitri moved to stand but froze at the man's stare.

"Ash." Leah's voice was soft and warm. "He's ok. He just wants to go back to the inn. He won't leave town. Not yet. He needs to know how much Tameer told her before he can run away."

Shit shit shit. She might not be a mind reader, but she definitely had him figured out.

SIX

Against her better judgment, Irena agreed to meet the prince, and Tam had immediately left for Vexia to find and retrieve said royal. She didn't like relying on a male to maintain her power, but that was the world she lived in. Until her child was born, she was a figurehead and nothing more.

She prayed to the gods that her child was male. Not because she didn't want a daughter, but a son would enable her to fix this godsforsaken kingdom and leave him a thriving place to rule when he ultimately came of age and relieved her of her authority. Perhaps, in that time, she'd be able to rewrite the laws so that anyone could be ruler of the land, regardless of gender identity. Gods, that would be quite a feat.

Tam promised to return with her—potential—intended by week's end.

"Your Majesty, the council is waiting for you."

"Thank you, Nicolette," Irena replied with an exhausted sigh. Time to meet with her committee of ignorant men so they could tell her all the reasons why her initiative to provide indoor plumbing to the poorer areas of Ravendale was impossible.

If she were a man, they wouldn't even be second-guessing her. They'd just make it happen. Fucking assholes.

Dimitri had been surprised when Leah and Ash had let him simply walk out of their home and back to the inn. He'd been considerably more shocked when Tameer had found him two days later, in the inn's dining hall nursing his black tea while mulling over all of his terrible life choices.

"Hello there, old friend," the man said as he clapped Dimitri on the back and took a seat at the table. "It's been so long since we last spoke."

Dimitri raised an incredulous eyebrow at him. "Old friend, eh? I'm surprised you even recognize my face. We were rather intoxicated when we last met."

Tameer chuckled. "You were intoxicated. I was pleasantly buzzed and enjoying the company of an alarmingly attractive out-of-towner." He gave Dimitri an exaggerated wink then flagged the waitress, Isa, down and requested a fresh pot of tea and a second cup.

Dimitri said nothing as the woman catered to Tameer's needs, sitting back and watching the man, desperately trying to get a read on him. *What the hells was he up to? What was his angle?* Dimitri had long since learned that no one operated out of the goodness of their heart, because very few people had any real goodness in them. Most were operating—on some level—on a self-serving mission of some sort. He just needed to figure out what Tameer really wanted and how he could use that to his advantage.

Adding a spoonful of honey to his tea, Tameer eyed him curiously, seeming to size him up. Nodding to himself, as though Dimitri had passed some sort of test, he placed the spoon on his saucer and said, "I have a proposition for you."

Dimitri sat up a little straighter in his chair. He didn't want to offend this man, as Tameer had a lot of power over him right now. He knew Dimitri's true identity and he could make things very challenging for Dimitri if he chose. Still, he needed to be direct. "With all due respect, sir, I appreciate your interest, but I'm not attracted to men."

Tameer stared at him for a moment, mouth hanging open, then he barked a laugh so loud the innkeeper popped her head into the dining hall.

Dimitri felt heat rush to his cheeks. He didn't think it was funny, and he was slightly offended now that Tameer clearly believed any sort of attraction between them was *thoroughly* laughable.

Tameer wiped tears from his eyes and took a deep breath. "Gods, thank you. I needed that." Chuckling still, he took a long pull from his tea before speaking again. "I apologize for misleading you. While you are most definitely a beautiful man, and under different circumstances, I would be happy to have you in my bed. But that's not what I meant."

Dimitri sat back in his chair, trying to keep his cool. His mind was spiraling over all the different things Tameer might want from a prince in hiding. It could be anything, and Dimitri would be forced to make a very difficult decision: acquiesce to the man's requests, or go home and face whatever arranged marriage his mother had concocted.

Tameer set his teacup back on the table and pivoted to give Dimitri his full attention. "I want you to marry my sister."

Too expensive.

A waste of resources.

Not worth the effort.

Irena was seething as she paced the room. She'd stopped listening to her council's arrogant, ignorant words, but they were still yammering. How could it possibly be a waste of money or resources to improve the lives of their citizens? Healthier citizens mean happier citizens. Not to mention, healthier workers are more productive. Irena had tried that argument with the advisors, but they'd brushed it off saying that they had an abundance of workers already. Implying that letting some workers get sick and die was acceptable because they had an excess of potential workers to fill in for those who couldn't pull their weight.

Fucking self-righteous bastards. They didn't view the poor as humans. Just cogs in their damn factories. Easily replaceable.

"Get out," she finally snapped, breathing heavily with rage

flowing through her veins making her skin hot. "Get out of my sight!"

Her chief advisor, Gustave, gave her a quizzical look. "Your Majesty, are you feeling all right? We still have quite a lot to discuss about your plans."

Her plans. They had no interest in her plans except to shoot them full of holes and try to make her feel like an errant child in the process.

"Did I stutter?" Irena asked, her voice hard as steel. "You are fired. All of you. You clearly aren't open to the idea of progress and I'm not going to fight you any longer. Get out of my sight and out of my castle."

The men glanced around the room at each other, sharing a look of indignance. Evidently, they didn't think she had the power to fire them. Honestly, Irena had no idea, but it felt *really* fucking good to try.

Gustave shook his head, turning to the rest of the council he said, "Let us go. Her Majesty is drained and needs to rest. We will continue this conversation later."

The patronizing tone wasn't lost on Irena, but as the men filed out of the room, she couldn't bring herself to care. Their patriarchal bullshit was more exhausting than the human growing in her stomach.

Maybe Tameer was right after all. Maybe she did need a husband. Or, at least the appearance of one.

Dimitri nearly choked on his tea. "Sorry, come again? I must have misheard you. It sounded like you said you wanted me to marry your sister."

"Aye, that's exactly what I said." Tameer grinned, then selected a biscuit from the plate in the middle of the table. "I should add, she's also the queen and currently pregnant with the deceased king's child."

Dimitri's head was spinning. This man, an obvious criminal, was related to the queen and he seemed genuinely serious in his proposal. What the hells?

"You can't honestly expect me to believe that you are related to the queen. No offense, but you don't exactly strike me as royalty."

Tameer nodded and swallowed his biscuit, "Adopted sister, but still very much family. We grew up together on the streets of Ravendale. Me, Irena, and Leah. We were as thick as thieves." He added a cocksure grin at his own bad joke.

It took a moment for Dimitri to fully process Tameer's words. "The queen isn't royalty?"

Tameer scoffed. "She's the fucking *queen*, mate. She's royalty, just not by birth."

Dimitri's mind was struggling to keep up with all this. He looked into his empty teacup, desperately wishing it was filled to the brim with the ouzo from his homeland. Tameer was still talking. The queen used to be a street kid, then an inhabitant of the orphanage, then she ran the orphanage? That was where the king had found her. Dimitri hadn't known King Odker personally, but he'd heard some horror stories about the man. His mother had refused to even entertain the prospect of a marriage between Odker and Dimitri's sister, Dalia, after the rumors of what he'd done to his second wife had reached their shores.

"I appreciate what you're trying to do for your sister, I really do, but why me? Why on earth would you want *me* to marry your queen when I'm obviously not a reliable prospect? Hells, I'm here because I'm avoiding marriages my mother is attempting to thrust upon me."

Tameer grinned confidently as he sat back in his chair. "That's why this arrangement is perfect for you. Irena doesn't really want a husband, but her advisors are a bunch of ignorant old men who don't like taking orders from a woman. She needs a man at her side, serving as a glorified mouthpiece, until her child is born. If it's a boy, Irena will be crowned Queen Mother and you can call the wedding off. Then you can return home a heartbroken man. That should get your mother off your back for a while at least."

"And if it's a girl...?" Dimitri prompted.

Tameer waved off the question. "We'll burn that bridge if we come to it."

Dimitri leaned back in his chair, his mind a blur of possibilities. A fake betrothal. Nothing permanent, just a few months pretending to be in love with a queen, being the male voice her advisors seemed to require while otherwise having no true responsibilities. It really was an intriguing offer. And it would certainly get his mother off his case.

"All right, when do I meet this queen of yours?"

SEVEN

A raven was waiting for Irena when she returned to her chambers after dinner. Tameer would arrive in the morning with her potential fake fiance. Dimitri Aetos, second son and prince of Westera. According to Tameer, he was beautiful, incapable of holding his liquor, and brimming with a devil-may-care attitude.

Irena sighed, shuffling into her bathing room with Nicolette by her side. Without a word, the woman began untying Irena's corset and helping her remove the many layers of fabric that engulfed her each day. Nicolette hurried to the large copper tub and turned on the water, then returned to help Irena remove the excessive number of pins that were used to keep her long, caramel curls into a perfectly pristine chignon. Irena took the crown from her head once it had been freed from the long pins that held it in place and set it on the vanity before her.

It was the only piece of jewelry Odker had ever given her,

and she couldn't look at it without feeling as though it were a shackle weighing her down. Hideous, gaudy, and bulky, the thing was a massive hunk of gold covered in a rainbow of gemstones. It was as though the goldsmith couldn't settle on any one color or theme and therefore decided to use them all. It weighed a ton and made her head and neck ache every time she wore it, which thankfully wasn't often. She only forced herself to wear the damned thing during meetings with her council, in the hopes that its presence on her head would remind them that they were supposed to listen to her. It hadn't worked yet, but she was nothing if not eternally optimistic.

"The bath is ready, Your Majesty." Nicolette's soft voice drew Irena out of her dark reverie. Remembering the night Odker had crowned her publicly, then raped her in their marital bed. She was lucky she'd gotten pregnant so quickly. The Medicus had strongly discouraged intercourse after conception, arguing that it could be harmful to the child. The woman was the only female authority figure in the entire castle and Odker begrudgingly listened to her. She hadn't been entirely truthful, of course, Irena knew that. But she was grateful, nonetheless.

Walking into the bathing room, Irena slipped out of her thin chemise and into the steaming, rose-scented water. The tub was deep enough to serve as a swimming pool for small children and she easily managed to submerge her entire body, giant pregnant belly and all. Relaxing her head against the side of the tub, she allowed her thoughts to drift. Irena had never felt the loving touch of a man, only the overly aggressive violations of her husband. She was one of the lucky few to make it out of Ravendale's slums without having to peddle her body for coin. Tameer and Leah had made sure of that. They were both a couple of years older than her and had taken it upon themselves to keep her safe and protected. She was twenty-two when she married Odker. Twenty-two when he tore her virginity from her. Twenty-three when she hired Leah to kill him. It had been the best decision she'd ever made. The weight that had been lifted from her shoulders the moment that vile man took his last breath had been worth her weight in gold.

Although Leah had refused to take any coin for the job, she promised she'd take her payment out in snuggles from the baby once they graced the world with their presence.

Gods, she hoped that would be soon. Looking down at her swollen, stretch-marked belly, she couldn't imagine how it could possibly get any bigger. The midwife assured her that she had at least another two months before her little one would arrive, but Irena couldn't comprehend how big her body would get by then.

Growing a human is fucking weird, she thought as she placed her hands on her belly and felt a little kick in response. Smiling, she sat forward and took the lavender soap from the table beside the tub. In the beginning, Nicolette had offered numerous times to help her bathe. Irena had politely, but firmly, informed the woman that she was quite capable of cleaning herself.

Irena only slightly regretted that arrogance as she attempted to scrub her feet. Damn swollen belly. It made everything more complicated.

The morning sun came much quicker than Dimitri would have liked. He'd agreed to meet Tameer's queen-sister, but he wasn't looking forward to it. If the woman was having that much trouble finding a new husband, there must be something wrong with her. Not to mention, he had no desire to wed anyone. That was the whole reason he was hiding out in Vexia in the first place. He didn't *want* to get married. He wasn't sure he'd ever want to tether himself to another soul for eternity, and that was what marriage was meant to be. Dimitri had grown up in court life. He'd seen both ends of the marriage spectrum. Love matches were *incredibly* rare, so much so that most didn't even bother seeking them out.

His own parents had been a match made in political heaven, allying their two great nation-states into one powerful nation. Westera was still a young nation, but she was thriving. His older brother, Dante, had married the eldest daughter of an emperor, legitimizing their country in the eyes of the world. Theirs wasn't a love match, but it was a comfortable relationship. His brother cared for Grace as the mother of his children, even if he didn't love her. She was an excellent partner for him, managing his short temper when dealing with self-serving courtiers, and they had made three beautiful children together.

Dimitri couldn't bring himself to sign up for a political marriage, though. He had the luxury of choice, being the second son, and he desperately wanted to find love. Or at least the prospect of love through a marriage to someone he knew and cared for. Unfortunately, there was no such woman in his life. The only women he encountered were courtiers looking for a scandal and the women his mother threw at him who were only looking for a crown. He wanted a partner. Why was that such an unreasonable request?

Tameer was waiting for him at the reception desk of the inn, chatting with the innkeeper. He looked up as Dimitri descended the last steps. "Great! Let's get going. It's not polite to keep a queen waiting." He gave Maddie one last smile, slapped the desk twice in goodbye, and walked out the door. Dimitri trailed along behind him, wondering how he'd let himself get sucked into this mess in the first place.

Irena's mornings were all basically the same: wake up, get dressed with Nicolette's help, breakfast in the Solarium, meetings with her advisors where they would tell her all the things she can't do, lunch in the gardens, more meetings in which her advisors try to explain that improving the lives of their citizens would be detrimental to the country's overall well-being, dinner in the Great Hall with visiting dignitaries, courtiers, and various other fussy people who thought they were better than everyone else.

It was exhausting and she actively dreaded each and every day. So why the hells was she trying so hard to maintain her crown and authority?

She looked out her bedroom window as Nicolette finished tightening her corset. Children chased a ball through the mud puddles along the street. They were giggling and having a wonderful time, despite their threadbare clothes and utter lack of shoes.

They were why she was here. The children of this city, of this *country*, deserved better lives. Irena stood a bit straighter. She was their queen and she would do whatever it took to improve their lives. Even if it meant marrying—or at least pretending to marry—a stranger from another country.

A knock at the door drew her focus as Nicolette pinned that gaudy crown to her head. "Your Majesty, your brother is waiting for you in the Great Hall," the guard said as she pushed the door open.

I guess it's time to get this over with.

EIGHT

Ravendale was a nice enough city, Dimitri supposed. The complete lack of ocean views and salty air made him nostalgic for home, but he needed to get over that. He wasn't planning on marrying an ocean queen. Hells, he wasn't even sure he was going to follow through on this sham engagement, anyway. He was just here to meet the queen. That was all. Nothing had been promised yet.

Tameer led him through the castle gates and into the Great Hall, nodding to guards he recognized and flirting shamelessly with most of them.

"I thought you were a criminal," Dimitri wondered aloud.

"I was. I'm a stand-up citizen nowadays. Well, mostly." Tameer tossed a cocky grin over his shoulder at Dimitri. "But most of these guards arrested me at one point or another. They're quite the malleable sort, truth be told. A couple sexual favors here and there and they let me be. It was a fantastic arrangement when I was head of the Thieves Guild."

Dimitri froze as Tameer nodded to the guards standing post outside the Great Hall. "I'm sorry, what?"

Tameer looked back at him with the most confident and annoying smirk yet. "A story for another time, dear boy. The queen awaits."

Dimitri stared dumbfounded after the man for a long moment. What the hells had he gotten himself into?

One of the guards cleared their throat. "Will you be joining him, sir?"

Dimitri blinked and nodded. He took a few steps into the room and was hit with a sudden wave of awe and amazement that nearly knocked him off his feet.

She was the sea. Everything from home that he loved and desperately missed personified. Her hair was the color of the softest sand on his favorite beach with waves that reminded him of the water lazily lapping at the shore. Her smile was the warmth of the sun at midday. Her eyes. Gods, her eyes were the most captivating things he'd ever seen. With depth and color to rival his beloved ocean.

Dimitri was instantly lost in her gaze. He had no problem imagining how he'd convince her council that he'd fallen for her—he was fairly certain he'd lost all sense of logic and reason the instant she set those eyes on him. The hardest part was going to be leaving and forgetting her once all this was over.

Dimitri was sure it would take a tidal wave sent by the god of the sea himself to drag him away from this siren goddess.

Dropping into the lowest bow he'd ever attempted, he spread his arms wide and said, "It is an utter pleasure to meet you, Your Highness." Righting himself, he added, "How may I be of service to your majestic and most beautiful self?"

A look of annoyance flashed in her eyes and she turned from him and addressed Tameer at her side. "You didn't tell me he was a shameless flirt and obvious rake."

Tameer grinned at Dimitri. "I didn't know. He wasn't flirting with me and the bar was surprisingly light of fair maidens for him to woo."

Dimitri studied Tameer in this new light, sizing him up and weighing his worth. It was an appalling habit he'd developed during his time in his brother's court, but it was quite helpful when determining a person's usefulness.

Tameer seemed to have the queen's ear, as he stood beside her on the dais. She deferred to him, if only slightly, and he seemed quite protective over her. The queen's hand rubbed across her abdomen absentmindedly, drawing Dimitri's attention to it. Tameer had told him about the child and that its birth would determine if they needed to follow through with this wedding. Seeing the queen now, the woman he was meant to fake an engagement with, protectively covering her womb, he wanted more than anything to be the man who had placed that child within her. Who the hells was the father and how could he be as lucky as that man who'd been honored to share a bed with this siren goddess?

Irena looked down at the prince from her perch atop the

most uncomfortable throne known to man. He was beautiful, Tameer hadn't lied, but he also gave off an air of unearned confidence, like most royals she'd met. Still, there was something intriguing about him.

And it didn't help that he was fawning all over her. Irena hadn't had that sort of attention from anyone in over a year and it was quite nice.

"I would never lie to you, Your Majesty. Or attempt to mislead you." Dimitri clasped his hands behind his back, likely trying to appear more genuine. Irena couldn't help but notice the way his shirt pulled taut against his chest, practically showing off the strength underneath the fine silk. Heat flushed Irena's face when she forced her eyes back to meet his and saw a knowing smile on his cocky face. "Tameer proposed an alliance, of sorts, between the two of us. As a mutually beneficial solution to some troubles we both seem to be facing from our respective courts. Is that something you are interested in, Your Majesty?"

"Irena, please. I mean, if we're meant to appear betrothed, you should at least call me by my name." The words escaped her lips before Irena had a chance to think them through. *Shit.* She wasn't even sure this was the right choice, but what other options did she have? An uphill battle with her advisors every fucking day, only to have them ultimately ignore her decisions and go off to do whatever the hells they wanted?

No. A male counterpart would help her solidify her reign until the child was born. She could pretend to be betrothed for a couple of months. Dimitri seemed nice enough.

What's the worst that can happen?

"Does that mean you'll agree to an engagement, then?" Dimitri's smile lit up something warm within her, but Irena refused to look too closely at that. She wasn't in the market for a real relationship. She had a country to run and a child on the way. Dimitri was clearly flirting with her because that's just who he was. He couldn't possibly be truly interested in her. Hells, she's carrying another man's child. No man she'd ever met would have seen that and thought, "Yes, that's the girl for me."

Shaking her head, trying to will those intrusive thoughts from her mind, she said, "Yes. I accept your proposal."

Irena could practically *hear* Tameer's gloating smile as he stood half a step behind her chair.

"Technically, I haven't proposed yet," Dimitri smirked. "If it pleases Your Majesty, I'd like to explore your beautiful capital for a while this afternoon and join you for an intimate meal this evening."

Irena did her best to conceal her intrigue, simply nodding. Tameer offered to show Dimitri the ins and outs of Ravendale and the two quickly departed. Sitting back in her throne, she couldn't help but wonder if she'd just made the biggest mistake of her life.

"Where the hells are you going?" Tameer was practically running to keep up with Dimitri, but he was a man on a mission.

"I need to find something."

"Anything in particular?" Tameer asked, an edge of annoyance in his voice, mixed with curiosity. "And do we really have to *run* to find it?"

Dimitri sighed but slowed his steps. He couldn't propose without it. He wasn't sure they'd even have something to fit what he needed in this near-landlocked country, but he had to try.

Irena was everything he'd ever imagined in a partner and he wasn't going to fail her right from the start.

Ideally, he'd never fail her, but Dimitri was a realist. He just wanted to make her smile and take some of the weight from her heavily over-burdened shoulders.

Tameer led him through the districts of the capital until they reached the merchant's area. Dimitri quickly looked through shop windows, praying to the god of merchants that he'd find what he was looking for.

The sun was just beginning to disappear behind the roofs of the shops when he saw it.

"This is it," he whispered.

NINE

Dimitri convinced Tameer to take him to the kitchens, where he requested Irena's favorite foods. According to the chef, the young queen had been quite partial to anything with bacon, so they decided on bacon-wrapped chicken breasts, with a side of green beans cooked in bacon grease, mashed potatoes with bacon pieces on top, a summer salad, and chocolate covered strawberries for dessert.

After consulting with both Tameer and Irena's handmaiden, they decided to serve the meal in the observatory with a view of the stars.

Apparently, one of the late king's great uncles had been quite the amateur astronomer. He'd built a state-of-the-art observatory around a hundred years ago. The space was no longer cutting edge, but it still boasted stunning views and Dimitri wanted to ensure that this, their first meal together and the night he proposed, would be a night Irena would never forget.

Dimitri was assigned a set of rooms in the east wing of the castle, supposedly near the queen, although he hadn't been shown which doors led to her. He made sure everything was set and perfect in the observatory, leaving Tameer to handle the final details, and went to his room to change into the finery he'd purchased during their shopping excursion. He returned to the observatory just as the last rays of light were fading from faint lavender to a deep navy.

Admiring his handiwork, Dimitri adjusted their chairs a hundred times before putting them back where the staff had originally placed them. He was about to start rearranging their dishes when he heard the door open followed by the soft clicks of her heeled boots on the tile floor as his siren goddess entered the room.

Irena hadn't been to the observatory in months. When she'd first wed Odker, she'd been given a full tour of the castle and its grounds, but she rarely ventured this far from the nexus of the castle proper. All of her daily duties required her to spend the majority of her time in meetings.

Dimitri had outdone himself. The space was filled with twinkling lights and delicious scents. The roof was open to showcase the cloudless sky and diamond-like stars.

"My gods," she exhaled in a whisper. "It's beautiful."

"A dinner fit for a queen." Dimitri beamed proudly at her and pulled out a chair for her.

Irena settled into the chair just as Dimitri removed the silver lid from the platter in the center of the small table. Inhaling deeply, she let out a moan that was borderline indecent. *Bacon.* It was on everything. The potatoes were sprinkled with bacon, cheese, and chives. The chicken was wrapped in multiple thick slices of bacon. Even her salad had chunks of bacon in it.

"Your chef mentioned you've had quite the taste for bacon since becoming with child. I don't blame you," Dimitri said with a grin as he seated himself. "Bacon is absolutely delicious."

"I've always had a weakness for the stuff," Irena replied. "But the baby seems to feel it too and I just can't deny this little bug anything." She reached for the serving spoon to fill her plate, but Dimitri quickly brushed her off and took her plate, piling it high with everything.

"Goodness, I don't know about women in Westera, but I don't think I could possibly eat that much." She smiled warmly at him, accepting the plate nonetheless.

"Eat until you're full," he said with a shrug. "You are eating for two."

That was the second time he'd mentioned her child, but it hadn't seemed judgmental or rude. He seemed genuinely interested in the well-being of her child. It was odd. In her experience, men rarely wanted anything to do with children, especially not a child fathered by another.

Irena refused to let herself dwell on those sorts of thoughts. This was a temporary arrangement, after all. Dimitri didn't need to show an interest in her child, although it was sweet that he was being so thoughtful. She needed to focus on the moment and enjoy this while it lasted. A few more weeks and her child would be born and things would change forever.

"Tell me about yourself, Dimitri," she prompted. "What do you do for fun? What are your interests? What are your favorite foods?"

Dimitri pondered her question while he chewed a bite of his chicken. "Well, let me see. Westera, as you know, is a maritime nation. We are surrounded by the sea on three sides, and the capital is right at the tip of our peninsula. Most of my childhood was spent in or near the ocean. I desperately wanted to be a pirate when I grew up, but my mother forbade it. She said no child of hers was going to go off on violent seafaring adventures." He chuckled at the memory.

Irena grinned, imagining a young, curly-haired little boy, racing along the sand with a wooden sword threatening fair maidens and swashbuckling the air. "I'm so sorry you didn't get to live your dream," a hint of humor in her voice as she teased him.

"Ah, such is life." Dimitri's smile was quickly becoming one of her favorite things.

"I imagine you would have made an excellent pirate. Stealing treasure and hearts all over the world."

"Then it's for the best that I never set sail. I would have missed out on meeting the most gorgeous woman on the planet simply because she rules a landlocked country." The warmth in his gaze stirred a heat within her.

Irena looked away, taking a long sip of her ice water, trying to cool herself down.

The rest of their meal passed quickly, filled with casually comfortable conversation and unexpectedly heated glances. Irena tried to ignore the sudden attraction she felt toward this man she'd just met, attempting to convince herself it was just the pregnancy hormones and the feeling would pass.

When they finished their meal, Dimitri took their plates and set them aside, bringing out a second, considerably smaller platter from under the dining cart. The lid was practically frosted from the dwarven mechanics that kept the cart cool.

"Dessert, Your Highness," he said, placing the platter on the table before her and dramatically lifting the lid. A mountain of chocolate-covered strawberries awaited her. The chilled chocolate quickly began to glisten as the humidity from the warm air settled on them. On top of the dessert mountain sat a purple box, wrapped in emerald ribbon with a massive bow in the center.

"What's this?" Irena asked, reaching carefully to remove the box without disturbing the strawberries.

"Open it." Dimitri grinned, settling back into his chair.

Gently, she pulled the ribbon, unwrapping it from the box and setting it aside. Removing the lid, Irena stared in confusion at the odd contraption nestled in velvet cloth within the box. "Um... it's lovely?" she said, trying to hide her puzzlement.

Dimitri chuckled and reached for the box. "It's a sextant," he said matter-of-factly. He picked up the odd brass instrument and held it to his eye, then handed it to her, motioning for her to do the same. "It's a tool used by sailors and pirates to navigate the seas. In Westera, it's customary to gift your intended with a sextant. It's meant to represent a literal and metaphorical guiding point in the relationship. The proposer gifts it to the proposee as a way of saying 'You are my guiding force. Without you, I'd be lost. With you, I will forever be home.'"

That warm tingly feeling was back, rushing throughout her entire body as she gazed into the depths of his enchanting brown eyes. Gods take her. This man would be the end of her if she let him. Hells, she'd just met him and she was already falling head over fucking heels for him.

"It's a bit cheesy, I know," Dimitri added quickly and looked away, seeming to take her silence as something negative. "But it's tradition and what are we without tradition?"

Irena grabbed his hand, ignoring the shock that instantly shot through her body at the contact. She held his hand until his eyes met hers once more. "I think it's beautiful and the meaning behind it is romantic and wonderful."

His eyes flicked over her face, seeming to be searching for a hint of deceit or dishonesty. Finding none, his eyes settled on her lips for a moment, long enough for Irena to feel the heat of his gaze. She licked her lips self-consciously. His eyes seemed to darken at the movement, driving that heated tingle in her body to her very core.

Dimitri leaned forward, his eyes seeking hers and silently judging her reaction to his movements. Irena knew, if she gave even a hint of disinterest, Dimitri wouldn't push. This was her chance to set a boundary and keep this agreement between them strictly business.

Her rational mind told her boundaries would keep her heart safe. Irena knew she would fall for this beautiful, thoughtful, poetic man if she gave herself half a chance. She knew this would end badly. She *knew* she should pull away.

Instead, Irena felt her body lean in, closing the distance between them. The moment her lips met his, Irena sealed her fate.

TEN

If Dimitri had any doubt about his affection for the queen, their kiss burned it all away. The instant her lips touched his, it was as though a switch had been flipped in his mind and he suddenly knew the true purpose of his existence.

She was everything he'd ever need. Irena and the child in her belly would become his whole world, if she'd let him. He just had to convince her that this temporary arrangement should be made permanent. Preferably before the child was born. After the birth, the sex of the child would potentially change everything. If she had a son, she wouldn't need him to legitimize her reign. Dimitri knew she was it for him, but he wanted her to feel the same before she had the decision removed from her control. That meant he had less than two months to show her how right they were for each other.

He prayed to the goddess of fated romance that she would be on his side.

Irena felt a pulse race through her body as they kissed. A wave of power she'd never known that seemed to drive her closer and closer to Dimitri. It terrified her.

Irena had only ever had one man in her bed and he'd been a ruthless, violent bastard. She had the scars—emotional and physical—to prove it. Granted, she'd known what she was getting into when she married Odker, it hadn't changed the damage it had done to her.

She hadn't had any delusions of changing him or fixing him with her love. Irena had been solely focused on protecting the girls in the orphanage from becoming his next victims.

Now though? Now she had the power, the control, to stop things before they got out of hand. So why didn't she want to? Why, even now, hours after their kiss, in the bright light of morning, did she still feel the heat of his breath on her lips? The taste of him on her tongue?

Irena pressed her fingers to her lips, closing her eyes and allowing her mind to travel back to the night before when her entire world had flipped on its head.

She went about her morning routine in a daze. Nicolette dressed her and pinned that monstrosity of a crown back on her head as she finished a breakfast of scones and fresh fruit. Then it was time for endless meetings. Irena was only half listening as her so-called advisors told her all the ways she was failing as a queen. Her mind was elsewhere. It wasn't until she heard Gustave arguing against her public works project—indoor plumbing for the poor—that she sat up straighter and gave them her full attention.

"I apologize, Your Majesty," he said in a voice completely devoid of remorse. "It's just not possible. We don't have the funds to take on such a lengthy project at the moment."

Irena openly glared at the condescending bastard. He gave up trying to confuse her with the numbers it would take to fund the project. Irena was smart. She understood the cost of the project and she knew full well that it was completely possible, all they needed to do was tax the ultra-wealthy merchants a mere one percent of their gross income. The merchants would hardly notice a difference in their lifestyles and it would make a dramatic improvement in the lives of the less-well-off. But Gustave didn't see it that way. He was convinced that the poor were poor because they wanted to be. He often said if they didn't want to be poor anymore, they should work harder to improve their lives. Irena had long since given up on trying to explain how ignorant and flat *wrong* his logic was. One bout of sickness in a household could demolish a family and their livelihood. Even the middle-class families were one serious injury or illness away from the poor house. Gustave, however, could not be reasoned with. He was a stubborn ass and for some reason that Irena couldn't fathom, he was the fool in control of their funds.

"With all due respect," Irena said, filling her words with so much sarcasm and vitriol that it was a wonder the man was still standing. "The poor neighborhoods need this project. It will improve their lives a hundred times and therefore improve the entire economy of Ravendale. I can't keep explaining this to you, but it will happen."

Gustave gave her his classic nod and smile. The most patronizing thing he could possibly do. It was his way of attempting to pacify her as though she were a recalcitrant child and not the leader of their fucking country.

Maybe she should ask Leah to kill that bastard too...

Eleven

Dimitri spent the morning aimlessly wandering the halls of the castle and casually inquiring about the queen. He hadn't known much about her when he first arrived, but by midday, he felt like he knew everything.

Former street kid, saved from forced prostitution when Leah took Irena to a convent. She was raised by a sect of women who devoted their lives to Na'kashi—a maternal-type goddess and patron guardian of lost souls. After the convent, Irena moved into the local orphanage. She worked there as a teen, although her original duties were unclear. By the time she met King Odker, she was assistant to the house mother. According to the maids, Irena had placed herself in Odker's way, flirting with him until he lost all interest in the children and took her as his bride.

The more Dimitri heard about Odker, the more he wished the man were still alive just so he could kill him himself. The dead king was as vile a man as there ever was. Hells, the maids said he'd gone to the orphanage to find a *child bride* because the surrounding royals refused to send him any more of their daughters. Irena was a saint, a gods-sent saint. She knew the man was a monster and still, she put herself in his sights to save the children from his violence.

Apparently, Irena and Odker were wed within the week. The maids whispered in harsh tones about the first two months of their marriage. Irena had her own bedroom, but until she became pregnant, Odker forced his way in every night. One of the maids began detailing the gore she'd found in Irena's sheets one night when Irena's handmaiden appeared around the corner and silenced the girl with a firm look.

"Sir, Her Majesty requested lunch in the library today. She asked that I extend an invitation to you," the handmaiden, Nicolette, said to him once the other maids had been chased away.

"That would be lovely." He gave her a smile. Dimitri didn't want to get the girls in trouble for gossiping, he just wanted to understand his betrothed.

"Right this way." She gestured for him to follow her and led the way out of the servants' work area and into the castle proper.

Dimitri nodded. Lunch with his betrothed sounded like a wonderful way to spend his time. He quickly fell in step with the young woman. "I don't mean to gossip and I hope their tales didn't offend. I just want to understand who Irena is. She seems so special and capable. I can't imagine she truly needs a man to rule this country."

"Tradition dictates that a man sits upon the throne." Nicolette's words were blunt and utterly devoid of emotion. Dimitri got the feeling that tradition didn't impress her much.

Dimitri grunted in response, but kept his thoughts to himself, for now. Irena needed him to be a silent male figurehead while she took control of her country. He could be that for her.

He would be anything for her.

The library wasn't a room traditionally meant for food, but it was Irena's favorite place. The peaceful serenity of the space was the perfect place for her to recharge after a series of bullshit meetings, before going back for another round of bullshit meetings after lunch.

She opened the excessively tall door to the library and was greeted by the scent of parchment, ink, and freshly baked bread. The entire north side of the room was nothing but crystal clear windows overlooking the small tributary that fed into the major river that bisected Mistfall and led to the sea. Beyond the slow-flowing water, mountains were just visible in the distance. Irena closed the door behind her with a firm click and fell back against the thick mahogany entry. Closing her eyes, she let out an exasperated sigh. Nothing in life should be as hard as it is to convince nine old men to relinquish funds to help their people.

"Hard day?" There was a hint of concern in Dimitri's voice

that instantly warmed Irena's heart.

Opening her eyes, she pushed off the door and accepted his proffered hand. She was surprised to find his hands weren't soft and smooth, like typical royals. There were callouses and scars decorating his strong hands. He gently wrapped her arm around his and escorted her to the table set for their lunch. She fought the urge to place her head on his shoulder and unload all of her problems. They just got engaged last night. They hadn't even announced it to her people yet, not to mention it would all come to an end in a couple of months.

He released her hand and pulled out a chair for her, then set about filling her plate. Grapes, warm, buttered bread, thick slices of honeyed ham, a large heaping of green beans—with bacon!—and a tall glass of sun tea. Once he made his own plate, he sat down beside her and asked again, "Has it been that bad a day already? It's the first day of our betrothal. I'd hope it would be a happy one." There was warmth and kindness in his words as he studied her face.

"I'm genuinely happy about our engagement, I promise. It's just nonsense with my advisors." Irena tried to wave off the topic and was about to ask him about his morning when he interrupted.

"Do you want to talk about it?" He was so open and genuine that Irena couldn't help it. As much as she wanted to keep boundaries between them and handle this bullshit on her own, she was *exhausted* and needed help. Hells, that was the whole reason she'd agreed to this sham engagement anyway, wasn't it?

"My advisors." Irena stabbed her ham a little rougher than was necessary, taking her knife and aggressively cutting off a piece of the meat. "They seem to think that because I'm a woman, I'm incapable of making sound decisions. They openly defy my requests and question my every move. Gustave"—she violently stabbed a roll, imagining it was the old fool's face—"is hells-bent on ruling this kingdom and is such an arrogant, condescending bastard." Irena didn't realize how truly pissed she was until she saw the damage she'd wrought on her poor, unsuspecting roll. The bread had been stabbed to bits and crumbs had flown across the table. "Shit," she muttered. Taking a deep, calming breath, she carefully put her fork down and shifted to face Dimitri head-on. "I'm sorry. That was needlessly violent of me. I promise I'm a perfectly sane person most of the time. That man and his cronies just push every one of my buttons."

Dimitri watched her closely, seeming to choose his words carefully before opening his mouth. Irena was silently impressed. Not many men in her life took the time to think before they spoke. It was refreshing.

"Your advisors are fucking idiots."

Irena choked on her tea at his bluntness.

"I wasn't sure what I thought you'd say, but that definitely wasn't it," she replied once she finally stopped coughing.

Dimitri shrugged. "It's the truth. If they can't see how smart and capable you are, they're fucking morons. My mother ruled Westera for nearly two decades after my father died and before Dante was old enough to take over. It was the most prosperous time in our country's history. Hells, my brother still goes to her for advice most days. Women have a unique perspective on things. Not to mention, at least in my experience, they are much more level-headed and slow to violence than men."

Irena sat back in awe. He'd said it. He'd actually said the things she'd been thinking for weeks but hadn't even attempted to vocalize. Men *were* quick to use violence as a solution. Odker had public executions almost daily and was constantly planning attacks on his supposed rivals over perceived insults. Most of which weren't even insults, he was just an over-sensitive baby who used violence to express all of his feelings.

"I know it's none of my business, seeing as I'm only meant to be here for a short time," Dimitri caught her eye as he said that. Irena got the impression that he wanted to say something about the impending expiration of their betrothal, but he seemed to change his mind. Instead, he finished with, "If you'd like me to come to any of these meetings, even just as silent moral support, I'd be happy to help you in any way I can."

Irena contemplated this for a moment, popping a grape into her mouth and chewing both the offer and the fruit over. Nodding, she agreed. They'd have to announce their engagement anyway, might as well do it in her meetings that afternoon. Perhaps then, her advisors would get their heads out of their own asses and start taking her seriously.

While Irena hated that she needed a man by her side for her advisors to listen to her, she was grateful that it was Dimitri. He seemed genuinely interested in supporting her reign without exerting power or authority of his own.

Dimitri hadn't really expected Irena to take him up on his offer for moral support, but he was thrilled when she did. She looked exhausted and utterly drained, and it was only midday. He couldn't imagine her afternoon meetings would go any smoother than her morning ones.

Dimitri couldn't explain it, even to himself, but he felt an overwhelming desire to protect her peace. Irena was a kind, thoughtful woman, and she deserved to be treated with the same level of care that she gave others.

After their meal, she led him back to the room where her advisors were already back at work. From the sounds of it, Irena wasn't thrilled that they started without her.

She grumbled something under her breath, but Dimitri couldn't understand it. Before he could ask her to repeat it, the guards on either side of the entryway pulled open the doors and she strode into the room.

Silence fell heavy in the air as she crossed the space and took her seat at the head of the table. Dimitri followed behind her, standing half a step back and to the right of her chair.

"Excuse me, sir," a balding, liver-splotched man addressed him with all the politeness of a crab caught in a fishing net. Which was to say the man was snappy and clearly not interested in conversation. "This is a private meeting. You can't be here."

Dimitri opened his mouth to reply, but Irena spoke first. "Actually, Gustave, he has as much a right to be here as any of us. I'd like to introduce you all to Prince Dimitri Aetos of Westera. My betrothed."

Dimitri was fairly certain he heard their jaws drop and several eyes nearly popped out of their skulls. This wasn't the news they'd been expecting. Poor, dumb bastards. He gave them all his most winning smile and a half bow. "It's a pleasure to meet all the men who assist my beloved in running this beautiful country."

It took a few—long and awkward—moments for the men to catch up and close their gaping mouths. They all quickly looked to the man Irena had addressed as Gustave. He looked as though he was struggling to maintain control of his anger. His pale face was flushed a startling shade of red and he was practically vibrating with barely contained rage.

"Your Majesty," he growled through gritted teeth. "You can't just get engaged without talking to us first."

Irena scoffed. "This was *your* idea, Gustave. You told me I needed a man by my side to temper my foolish female whims." Her words were dripping with sarcasm and condescension. "I'm simply doing as you advised. Isn't that what you wanted?"

Irena plastered an obviously fake smile on her face, giving off the air of an accommodating woman while showing off the authority her crown and title afforded her. It was breathtaking.

"Your Highness, we meant for you to pick someone we'd already vetted for you." Gustave tried to maintain a cordial tone, but he wasn't succeeding.

"You mean you wanted me to pick someone who would let you run this place into the ground. Squandering all our wealth and continuing the abuses on our people." Irena's tone was impressively level and calm as she called her advisors out for their bullshit.

Dimitri leaned casually against the side of her chair, eyeing the men and enjoying the looks of discomfort and fear that filled their eyes. It was exhilarating to see his queen at work.

"I'm sorry if you feel cheated out of usurping my crown, but with all due respect, I don't give a damn." Irena sat straighter in her chair, leaning forward and locking eyes with each and every one of the men in turn. "You are more than welcome to quit. Otherwise, we have work to do."

She waited a few seconds, giving the men just enough time to weigh their options before she sat back again, hands resting on her belly once more. "Now that that's settled," she continued, "we need to get back to our plan for indoor plumbing in the lower-income neighborhoods."

A collective groan escaped the men as they openly rolled their eyes. Gods, these men had the audacity to *openly* disrespect their queen? No wonder she was exhausted. She wasn't just struggling under the weight of ruling, but fighting an uphill battle constantly just to get her advisors to listen to her.

The gods had clearly sent him here for a reason.

Dimitri stepped forward, placing a comforting hand on Irena's shoulder and raising an eyebrow in question. *Is it all right if I say something?* he silently asked.

She waved her hand in a *Give it a shot* gesture and Dimitri addressed the men. "I'm sorry, gentlemen, I haven't been briefed on all the goings-on in Ravendale. What is the issue with the indoor plumbing in the low-income neighborhoods?"

The men glanced around the table, looking at each other and ultimately Gustave who was too busy grinding his teeth and glaring at Irena to respond. One of the men, slightly younger than the rest but still at least sixty, replied, "Um, well, Prince Dimitri, there isn't any."

Dimitri feigned shock. He, of course, already knew this after his lunch with Irena, but it was better to play dumb with these types and let them think they were making the decisions while he was actually the one leading them where he wanted. "That can't be! A country as prosperous and thriving as Mistfall doesn't even have indoor plumbing for all the residents of the capital? How is that possible?" He focused his attention on Gustave then, drawing the man's ire for a moment before he seemed to blink it away. Interesting. Dimitri was always suspicious of those who could mask their rage so well. He also thought it was noteworthy that the head advisor only masked his rage while looking at Dimitri. He didn't bother with such courtesy for his queen. *He doesn't respect or even acknowledge her authority.*

"It's an incredibly expensive and labor-intensive endeavor, Your Royal Highness. The funds simply aren't available." Gustave kept an impassive tone, almost hiding the annoyance he clearly felt at having to address this topic once more.

"Does the kingdom pay you for your advice, sir?"

"Of course. I'm the queen's most trusted and experienced advisor." Gustave sat up a little straighter.

"So you must make a pretty penny then."

The man puffed his chest, feeling unjustly proud of his position.

"My queen has expressed a desire to improve the lives of her citizens. If it's true that the coffers are so low that such an endeavor isn't feasible, then perhaps we should simply take the money from your salary. You seem more than content to show off your wealth." Dimitri gestured to the man's gaudy, gem-encrusted robes and excessive gold jewelry. "Perhaps our queen pays you too much and that money could be put to better use elsewhere."

The silence that followed was deafening. Dimitri wondered if he'd crossed a line until he heard Irena fail to stifle a laugh.

Gustave's face turned the most brilliant shade of red as he fought his rage. Lashing out at the queen's intended would not serve him well. The other advisors shifted uncomfortably in their chairs, nervously glancing around the room, looking anywhere but at them.

Irena, seeming to have gotten a handle on herself, chimed in. "I think that's a brilliant idea, love." She offered him a glowing smile that left Dimitri slightly dizzy. "Perhaps we should cut the salaries of all my so-called advisors. I imagine a fifty-percent cut would easily cover the cost of indoor plumbing for the homes in our poorest neighborhoods." She leaned forward, visibly excited by this idea. "If we cut them by seventy-five percent, I imagine we could get them new roofs as well. Oh, I love this idea!"

All of the advisors turned their anxious eyes toward Gustave, obviously expecting him to stop this somehow. Dimitri's grin widened as he watched the man struggle to maintain his composure. That asshat had insisted on Irena taking a husband to rule. Well, she had a man by her side now and she was going to get what she wanted or he'd die trying to give it to her.

"Perhaps we can find it in the budget elsewhere," Gustave said through gritted teeth. "I shall meet with the bookkeepers post haste and see what we can come up with."

Irena beamed at Dimitri for a moment but seemed to catch herself and a mask of polite indifference slipped back over her face. "You do that," she said to Gustave. "But if you can't find a way, know that I have no qualms about the plan my intended proposed. It will get done, one way or another."

Gods, she was stunning when she used that strong, authoritative tone. Seeing those advisors cower at her sent a rush of heat through his body. She was a goddess, all right. The goddess of vengeance and justice.

Twelve

I rena was practically giddy with power after watching Gustave and the others squirm. It was *exhilarating*. The meeting came to a quick conclusion after Dimitri's clever tactic, with her advisors filing out of the room while throwing glances back at her and Dimitri. Some of their eyes were filled with worry, most seemed irritated with hints of anxiety. Only Gustave seemed to be harboring serious anger and resentment.

The second the door closed behind them, Irena shot up from her chair and threw her arms around Dimitri's neck, practically tackling him with the unexpected gesture. He quickly threw his arms around her to keep them from falling.

"That was amazing!" she cheered with unadulterated glee. "I've never seen them look so cowed and submissive. It was utter perfection."

Dimitri chuckled into her hair but didn't release her. "That man is fixated on his wealth and authority. Threaten to take that away and you'll have him by the balls. It's all about finding the right tactic, love."

Irena stiffened at his use of the word *love* but she tried not to read too much into it. Hadn't she just used the same term of endearment when addressing him before her advisors? Although she'd meant it more in a performative manner and there was no one here for Dimitri to be performing for now...

Seeming to sense her struggle, he loosened his hold on her, allowing her the opportunity to escape his embrace if she wanted.

Gods help her, she didn't want to. There was something so calming and comforting about being wrapped in his arms. He smelled of citrus and salt. Perhaps that was just the sea in his blood. Irena had never been to Westera, but maybe she should. If the whole place smelled as magical as Dimitri, she might never want to leave.

Dimitri could have stood like that with Irena for the rest of eternity. The feel of her soft body flush against his own, the smell of her surrounding him, and the gentle kick of her child... It was heavenly. But she'd tightened when he'd called her love. He regretted it the instant he'd felt her body tense. Not because he didn't feel it, but because he'd made her uncomfortable.

In all honesty, Dimitri wasn't sure if what he felt for her was in fact *love*, but he didn't bother trying to deny the strong affection he felt toward her and the instinct he had to protect her and her child.

A soft cough sounded through the room. Dimitri lifted his head from where it had been resting atop Irena's hair to see Nicolette quietly waiting at the door. "Apologies, Your Majesties. Queen Irena, the mother of the orphanage is here, as you requested."

"Shit," Irena muttered into his chest. Dimitri was surprised that she hadn't pulled away when Nicolette entered the room. Maybe she wasn't as uncomfortable as he thought. "I completely forgot about that."

"Do you need help with it? Would you like me to come along?" Dimitri had no idea why Irena had summoned the mother of the orphanage, but he wasn't ready to part from her side just yet.

Irena pulled away a little, her arms loosening their grip while her fingers moved to play with the hair at the nape of his neck. It took everything in Dimitri to keep from openly shivering at her touch. Dimitri wasn't sure if she knew the effect she was having on him, until she tugged her bottom lip between her teeth, her gaze fixating on his lips. *Oh, yeah, she definitely knew what she was doing.*

Blinking suddenly, Irena released him and stepped back.

"Thank you for the offer, but I should probably do this one alone. It's a more sensitive issue and I'm not sure she'd be comfortable discussing it in front of a man, much less a stranger." Irena took his hands in hers and squeezed them. "Seriously, thank you. For being here. For helping me put those jackasses in their place. For being so willing to go along with this whole farce."

Farce. Right. They were just supposed to be pretending to be in love and engaged. Dimitri needed to get his head on right. He wasn't actually going to marry this woman. He had to stop letting his imagination run wild.

"We should make a formal, public announcement. Telling your advisors was great and all, but it doesn't solve my problem." Dimitri tried to keep a cool tone, but he felt himself disconnecting. It was a self-preservation technique he'd learned as a child. A way to distance himself from the rumors and cruel words whispered about him when the courtiers thought no one was listening. Dimitri needed to keep a safe distance from this woman. For all they knew, she was currently growing the next king of Mistfall and wouldn't need him around much longer.

As much as he wanted to be the one to protect Irena and guard her peace, he needed to prioritize his own emotional well-being. He couldn't let himself fall in love with a woman when the relationship had a definite expiration date.

Thirteen

I rena felt it. The moment Dimitri began to pull away and put space between them. Mental and emotional space although not physical. They made a public announcement of their intent to marry from the balcony overlooking the courtyard of Ravendale, as well as sending out announcements to all the other kingdoms on the continent, as was tradition.

The next few weeks were a blur of meetings, receiving gifts, and delaying wedding plans. While her advisors had *magically* found the funds to begin the in-door plumbing initiative, Gustave was now constantly badgering her about setting a wedding date. Irena got the impression that he didn't fully believe their engagement was real. Truthfully, though, it didn't matter what he thought. Irena was queen and she wasn't going to give that up without a fight.

"Everything looks wonderful, Your Highness," the midwife said and Irena retied the robe around her belly. The midwife had begun visiting her once a week, checking her progress and the baby's growth. "Your little one has turned and is head down, which is an excellent sign. Still no dilation, but that's to be expected. First-time moms tend to have longer pregnancies and slower births. I suspect it will be a few more weeks before they grace us with their presence."

Irena nodded, only half listening. While she was excited to meet her baby, she was dreading the birth. Depending on the sex of whomever exited her body, her fate with Dimitri was beyond her control. Despite the distance he seemed hells-bent on maintaining, she'd come to rely on his guidance and his skillful politicking. He'd been training for this job his entire life. She had no experience and a plethora of people trying to thwart her every move.

Gods, it would be easier if he just stayed. Maybe she should ask him to make their arrangement legitimate? As the midwife exited and Nicolette returned to help her dress for the day, Irena's mind wandered. She wondered what it would be like to wake beside Dimitri each day. Feel the warmth of his smile and the confidence of his presence as she navigated this strange world of courtiers and politics.

No. Irena shook her head, trying to rid herself of those thoughts. She couldn't ask Dimitri to give up his future just to accommodate hers. Even if he was the brightest part of her day and the one face she looked forward to seeing. He deserved to find love with someone who was trauma and entanglement-free. Someone who could freely give their heart to him without having to first reveal all their scars. Ideally, someone who wasn't about to give birth to another man's child.

It would be selfish of her to ask him to stay any longer than was absolutely necessary.

Dimitri never wanted to leave. Irena had quickly become the most important and awe-inspiring person he'd ever met and Dimitri could feel himself becoming a better person just by being near her. He desperately wanted to stay with her, marry her, and raise this baby with her. Maybe even have a few more babies. He'd never had much interest in fatherhood before, but watching the child grow in Irena's belly, feeling it squirm and kick, he didn't want to imagine a world in which he wasn't able to see this child learn to navigate the world at large.

He'd been trying to create some distance, protecting himself because he didn't want to get hurt when their engagement inevitably ended, but he was failing miserably. While he might have been able to create the appearance of emotional distance, she was all that filled his thoughts and dreams. His mind played scenes of what his life could be like if he stayed with her. Seeing the birth of her child. Holding her as she nursed the baby for the first time. Standing by her side as she introduced the babe to the citizens of Ravendale. Late-night feedings. Morning cuddles. Nights when the babe was finally sleeping through the night and he and Irena were given the chance to truly connect... physically.

Those were the best and worst dreams of all. Waking him with an arousal that refused to be ignored and a feeling of guilt.

He refused to take himself in hand and deal with the problem. It felt too much like using her, and Irena had been used enough to last a lifetime. If he were ever given the opportunity to satisfy his cravings for her, he would be *certain* to take care of her several times over before finding his own release.

Dimitri wandered the gardens in the eastern wing of the castle. His mind was off in another world, imagining what his life could be like if their engagement was real and not this charade designed to satisfy their respective problems. He didn't even see Tameer until he practically walked right into the man.

"Oh, gods!" He took a step back, running his hand through his hair and stumbling to give Tameer space. "I'm sorry. I wasn't looking where I was going."

"Or listening, apparently," Tameer teased. "I called your name three times before you attempted to mow me over. Everything ok?"

Dimitri forced a smile and nodded. "Aye, all's well. I was just thinking about some things and wasn't paying attention. What are you doing here?"

Tameer studied him for a beat, as though he wanted to ask more, but decided against it. "With the impending arrival of my first nibling, I've decided to live here in your fancy palace until the baby shows up. I'm impatient and waiting for ravens isn't nearly as thrilling as it sounds. Plus," he added with an air of annoyance. "Leah and her guard are getting a bit too vocal in their activities for my liking. I needed a break from all the graphic moans and screams." He shuddered dramatically and Dimitri couldn't help but laugh.

"I never took you for a prude," he teased.

Tameer gasped and swatted Dimitri's arm. "I am *not* a prude," he protested indignantly. "But when I've been awoken three times in one night to the sounds of my best friend crying out in blasphemous ecstasy? I need a reprieve. Judge not, my dear prince. You'd want to get away from them too."

Dimitri clapped him on the shoulder. "Well, I'm sure Irena will be happy to see you. And there's no chance for such late-night interruptions here, I promise you."

Tameer eyed him once more, subtly raising an eyebrow in question, but Dimitri chose to ignore it. He and Tameer were friendly enough, but he didn't know the man enough to bare his soul. Not to mention, Tameer and Irena were family. Anything he said to Tameer would definitely get back to Irena. As much as Dimitri wanted to stay and be at her side for the rest of his life, he couldn't ask that of her. She only agreed to pretend to marry him to buy herself time until the child was born. Irena wasn't truly interested in marrying him, just as he hadn't been truly interested in marrying her. Until he met her, anyway.

No. He couldn't tell Tameer how he was feeling. He wouldn't burden the man with foolish sentiments and dreams of a life with Irena.

Instead, he said, "Come, let's go find my betrothed. I know she'll be thrilled that you're here to stay a while."

"Tameer!" Irena's cry of joy echoed in the empty dining hall.

She abandoned the seating chart she'd been fighting with and waddled over to embrace her brother.

"Look at you," he beamed down at her, holding her at arm's length to take in the full image of her enormous belly.

Irena sighed, glancing down at her protruding stomach. "I know. I'm a whale. But just a few more weeks and I'll get my body back!"

Dimitri *tsk*ed beside Tameer. "You aren't a whale, my queen. You are a goddess and the walking embodiment of female divinity."

Heat flushed her face and she couldn't bring herself to meet his gaze. Dimitri had such a way with words. Irena was certain if he hadn't been born a prince, he would have become an internationally renowned poet or bard.

Tameer gently placed a finger under her chin and tilted her head until her eyes met his. "I don't normally like to agree with royalty, but the prince is right. You are *stunning*." He took her hand and twirled her around, making her giggle like a child. Irena could feel the heat of Dimitri's gaze on her as Tameer pulled her into his arms and danced across the room. She tried to ignore it, but the weight of his eyes sent a shiver down her spine. "We need to talk." Tameer's whispered voice in her ear sent an entirely different shiver down her spine.

Those words never preceded good news.

Irena let Tameer lead her back across the room to where Dimitri stood watching, a small grin tugging at his plush lips. With one final turn, Tameer released her and took a dramatic bow.

Despite her massive belly, Irena returned his bow with a curtsy and a glowing smile. Dimitri leaned against the table she'd been sitting at when they arrived and nodded to the paperwork she'd been struggling with. "What are you working on? Can I help at all?"

That was quickly becoming Dimitri's motto, as far as Irena could tell. He was always quick to offer his aid. Loathe as she was to admit it, having him by her side had made her entire life considerably easier. He took on all the tasks she dreaded, as well as offering insightful advice to assist her in navigating the drama of court life. He had made himself utterly irreplaceable and Irena couldn't help but hope her child was a girl, just so he'd have a reason to stay.

"Gustave insisted we start the wedding plans. This is the list of guests he claims we have to invite or risk international incidents. However, many of these families don't get along for one reason or another, so he recommended a seating chart. For some reason, he's of the mind that a seating chart falls under my list of duties as queen." Irena rolled her eyes, annoyance flowing off her in waves. That man really was trying to do everything he could to drive her insane.

Dimitri picked up the list and flipped through it. "I can handle this if you'd like. I've known most of these families my whole life. I know which ones shouldn't be seated together. Unless you'd like our wedding to devolve into an all-out brawl." A glint of something bordering on impish twinkled in his eye. "Although, I wouldn't mind seeing some of these people fight. It might bring them down a peg or two."

Irena gave him a faux-chastising look. "We can't have a fight in the middle of the ceremony."

Dimitri exhaled dramatically. "Whatever you say—"

"We should at least save that level of entertainment for the reception afterward."

The silence that followed her words dragged on for so long that Irena began to question if she should have said it at all. Then Dimitri's face broke out into the most beautiful smile as his guffaw echoed in the room. Tears glistened in his eyes while he struggled to maintain his composure.

Tameer chuckled and muttered something about bringing Leah along next time, but Irena wasn't really paying attention to him. Her attention was entirely fixated on the gorgeous man pretending to be her betrothed and the way his laughter filled her heart with warmth.

Gods, save her. She was falling for her fake fiance.

Fourteen

I rena and Tameer left Dimitri to fight with the seating arrangements for the wedding that wouldn't actually happen. Irena asked Nicolette to bring fresh tea and snacks to her sitting room and she and Tameer got comfortable. Irena tried to ignore the anxious feeling that had been building in her chest since he'd said they needed to talk, but she dropped the act now.

"What's going on? What's wrong? Is Leah ok? Ash? I know I said I'd pardon him, and I intend to, but my fucking *advisors* aren't letting me do much of anything these days."

"Breathe, darlin'. It's nothing like that. We're all fine and well. Although, their nocturnal behaviors have been happening at all hours more and more and I'm sick of it. I was actually hoping to stay here with you for a while. At least until my little nibling makes their arrival."

Irena collapsed into an armchair on an exhale. "Is that all? Of course you can stay here! I thought something was *wrong*."

She kicked her foot at him, missing his leg by several feet. "Don't scare me like that. Fuck. You're gonna push me into early labor."

Tameer chuckled and took a seat across from her. "Apologies, Your Highness. I didn't mean to upset you." He studied her for a moment, then added, "Would labor be the worst thing right now? If my nibling turns out to be a nephew, then this whole marital farce can be called off and you can go back to business as usual."

Irena could tell Tameer was hinting at something, but she couldn't pinpoint what it was. Instead, she opted to answer his question directly. "The midwife says it could be any day now, but I don't feel ready. Although I imagine I'll never really feel ready. You can only prepare so much for such a life-altering event."

Tameer nodded sagely, but there was a glint of humor in his eyes. "I get that, but that's not really what I meant. If your child is a boy, you'll be free of Dimitri. I know you weren't thrilled by the prospect of marriage again. I imagine it would be quite liberating to release him from your sham engagement." He watched her intently, trying to get a read on her reaction.

Irena wanted to agree; being able to rule on her own had been her intention ever since she'd contracted Leah to kill Odker months ago. Now, however, she found the idea of being alone—or rather, being without Dimitri—to be considerably less desirable.

Dimitri handled the seating chart with ease. His mother had insisted that all of her children learn the art of balancing different personality types, as part of their royal training. He was a skilled negotiator, an excellent small-talker, and a practiced problem-solver. All things he'd put to good use in the last few weeks to make himself as useful as possible to Irena.

He wouldn't be here forever; he'd accepted that fact. But he'd be damned if he left her without having done every conceivable thing to improve her day-to-day life. Which was why, after he'd finished the seating arrangements, he'd gone off in search of Nicolette.

He found her in the kitchens, informing the cooks that they needed to add Tameer to their meal planning for the foreseeable future.

Dimitri waited at the door, not wanting to interrupt or distract them. Unfortunately, in doing so, he successfully scared the crap out of the young woman.

Nicolette clutched her chest and stifled her cry when she recognized him, but Dimitri immediately felt guilty. "Apologies," he said with a bow. "I didn't mean to startle you. I was just hoping to get your advice on a few things."

To her credit, Nicolette bounced back from her fright quickly, nodding and motioning for Dimitri to join her as she exited the kitchens and made her way down the hall. "Of course, Your Highness. How may I be of assistance?"

"I'm sure you've seen how our queen has been treated by her advisors," Dimitri began. He didn't want to manipulate Nicolette into helping him do something that might be considered borderline treasonous, but he knew she cared for Irena. Playing on that seemed like the safest bet. When she only nodded, he continued. "I'm hoping to find a lesser-known rule in your laws that would give her leverage over them. Especially Gustave." Dimitri didn't bother hiding the distaste he felt toward the man, knowing that if Nicolette truly cared for Irena—as he suspected she did—she would likely feel the same disdain for Gustave.

Nicolette didn't skip a beat. She did, however, pivot rather unexpectedly causing Dimitri to stumble or risk trampling the woman. Again. She eyed him suspiciously. "How can I be sure you aren't looking into our laws to find a way to usurp our queen's power?"

It was a valid question, and one Dimitri had been prepared for. Nicolette might be a handmaiden, but she had spent the majority of her life in court and knew the conniving ways of royals. Raising his hands to show his innocence, Dimitri said, "I would never do anything to cause her pain or strife. I'm only interested in helping her achieve her goals. You are more than welcome to join me in my research endeavors. Your assistance would be greatly appreciated."

Dimitri could practically *feel* Nicolette's eyes tearing him apart. Looking for any hint of deceit or treachery. She would find none. Dimitri may have been a self-serving prince with an appetite for a new lady every night, but the instant he'd seen

Irena, something in him had changed. Like a missing puzzle piece finally fitting into place. He would never do anything to harm her.

Seeing the truth of his words in his eyes, Nicolette's posture relaxed a bit. "I'm not sure if I can help you find what you're looking for, but I know where to look. The laws and standards of our country are well documented and kept in our legal library. Technically, I don't have access to that room, but as the queen's betrothed, I imagine you won't have any problems gaining access."

"They keep the books locked away?" That seemed ridiculous. What threat could words on a page truly pose? However, he intended to use those very books to dispose of some rotten fruit in the queen's advisory council.

"Yes, Your Highness. For as long as I can remember, certain books, and books on certain topics, have been removed from the public areas." Nicolette kept her tone even, but Dimitri got the impression that she didn't agree with this tactic.

"Who decides which books get placed in these special libraries?"

Nicolette gave him a pointed look and he instinctively knew what she was going to say before she opened her mouth. The advisors. They probably had any book pulled that they didn't like or agree with. Fucking selfish pricks. Hiding anything that might give the people a chance to think or fight for themselves.

"Take me to this library, please. I have some reading to do."

Nicolette hadn't been exaggerating when she said the books were under lock and key. Armed guards stood watch on either side of the thick mahogany and iron doors. They refused Nicolette entry, as she'd warned Dimitri they would, but after playing the "I'm the queen's fiance and your future king" card, they stepped aside and allowed him to bring Nicolette in with him.

The room was stale and dark. An interior room with no windows and minimal candlelight. Hells, Dimitri ended up going back to the guards and requesting they send for three candelabras and some firewood. Not only was the room stuffy, but it was decidedly cooler than everywhere else in the castle. It was early spring and the cold stone walls did little to embrace the warmth of the sun. Several minutes later, a knock on the library door informed him that their supplies had arrived.

The guards steadfastly refused to let the servant enter the library to start the fire, so Dimitri carried the wood himself and burned an embarrassing number of matches before the fire finally took hold. The soft crackling of the logs brought an ambiance to the depressing room that it was sorely needed. Nicolette lit the candelabras, placing them strategically on a long table that sat in the middle of the room.

They each took a single candle from the decorative lights and wandered off into the stacks. If there was a system to the books, Dimitri couldn't identify it. It was as though someone had randomly thrown books onto the shelves without care, locking the door behind themselves and never looking back.

Truthfully, that was probably *exactly* what had happened.

"I found something!" Nicolette called from across the room. She emerged from a shadowy corner, a hefty tome in one hand, her candle in the other. Dimitri met her at the table and pulled one of the bright candelabras closer.

She laid the massive book on the table, opening it to the page she had marked with her finger, and turned it to face him. "This part talks about removing council members. Supposedly, the title is meant to be a lifetime appointment, but there are a few—very specific—instances in which a council member can be removed from office."

Dimitri skimmed through the section she pointed to, then went back over it more thoroughly. A fox-like grin spread across his face as a plan began to formulate in his mind.

FIFTEEN

"You're both fucking idiots."

Irena gaped at Tameer. He was always blunt and to the point, but damn. That seemed excessively harsh. "What are you talking about?"

"You and Dimitri, obviously. I've been watching you two all week. You're in *love* with him. Hells, a blind, deaf mute could see that you two are crazy about each other and yet here you are, preparing to give birth without him. Planning a future without him. Fully intending to end this perfection of an engagement that *I* designed. Fucking idiots."

"The engagement was always supposed to end, Tam. Or do you not remember the plan that *you* orchestrated?" Irena exhaled sharply as her stomach tightened. "Now, if you don't mind, I'm kind of in the middle of something here."

She waved Nicolette over. "Fetch the healer and the midwife."

With a quick bow, the woman was out the door in a flash.

Tameer, however, was still casually lounging on her chaise, completely oblivious to the scene playing out before him.

Irena gripped the back of a chair as another contraction washed over her. Gritting her teeth, she tried to breathe through it but ended up swearing like a sailor instead. "Who the fuck decided women had to be the ones to birth the babies, huh? What arrogant *man* thought this bullshit up?"

Tameer, finally reading the room, came to her side and took her hands to guide her to the settee. "I believe that was the goddess of creation. Not a man, unfortunately. I suppose they felt like they needed a balance in this process. Yes, the females of the species are the only ones with the power to create life, but it has to be painful so you don't let that power get to your head." Irena squeezed his hands until she felt his bones grind together and he let out a whimper. "I could be wrong though," he muttered. "It was probably an idiot man who didn't like the idea of women having too much power."

Nodding her agreement, Irena collapsed into the chair. "Sounds right," she groaned as the contraction subsided. "Fucking arrogant man."

Tameer knelt before her, lifting her feet and laying her legs out on the settee. "Do you want me to summon him? I can't imagine he'd want to miss this."

Irena didn't want to admit that she was scared. That the idea of Dimitri being by her side during all this brought her immense comfort. She didn't want to depend on him. She couldn't. He'd be leaving sooner rather than later. She needed to be able to do this on her own. After all, she was going to be on her own for everything else.

She couldn't bring herself to vocalize how she was feeling, so she just shook her head and took a deep breath as the next wave of pain crashed over her.

The sound of footsteps running down the hall froze Dimitri in his tracks. He looked down the hall just in time to see Nicolette, the healer, and the midwife disappear behind the door to Irena's rooms.

"Fuck," he whispered under his breath, then he broke into a run, reaching the door before it even clicked closed.

Irena was stretched out on the chaise lounge, Tameer holding her hands, as the midwife knelt beside his queen and placed two fingers on Irena's neck, checking her pulse.

Dimitri raced across the room and practically slid on his knees to her side. "What's going on? Are you ok? Is she ok?" He addressed the midwife with his last question, taking Irena's hand in his and anxiously studying her face as though he might be able to see the answers to his questions in her eyes.

As the midwife moved to the end of the chaise and lifted Irena's dress up over her knees, Irena's grip on Dimitri's hand reached a bone-crushing intensity. She ground her teeth and seemed to be trying to swallow her agony-filled cries with minimal success.

"Deep breaths, Your Majesty," the midwife said to Irena,

seeming to ignore Dimitri's rather stupid questions. It was obvious, as he knelt beside her, that she was, in fact, *not* ok.

Irena tried to follow the woman's direction, taking as deep a breath as she seemed capable and exhaling hard.

"This is going to be a bit uncomfortable, Your Majesty, I'm sorry. But I need to check the babe's positioning. All right?" The midwife didn't actually wait for Irena's reply. She had one hand under Irena's skirt and the other atop her stomach, feeling around for something.

Irena gave up all pretense and cried out in such agony that Dimitri felt compelled to draw his weapon and slaughter whatever caused her such pain.

"The baby is in the perfect position, Your Highness." The woman was smiling. Smiling?! While Irena was clearly suffering unimaginable pain, this fucking midwife was grinning like a fool. "How long have the contractions been like this?" She addressed the room and Dimitri felt like an utter asshole. She'd been in labor and he hadn't even known.

"About fifteen minutes," Tameer answered, holding Irena's other hand and brushing a stray lock of hair from her brow. "It just happened all of a sudden. We were talking and then she was screaming."

Dimitri wanted to smack the man. His beautiful goddess was attempting to bring life into this world. How could he be so glib?

The midwife seemed unfazed by Tameer's nonchalance, her hand reappearing from under Irena's skirt. She took a small cloth and wiped her hands clean, then dropped it into a bag.

Retrieving a second clean cloth, she handed it to Nicolette and instructed her to wet it with cool water and return with a pitcher of ice water.

The door closed soundlessly behind the handmaiden as the midwife moved to stand. "I'm afraid you aren't having this baby today."

Stunned silence filled the room, followed by a sharp inhale as Irena gripped his hand tighter once again.

"What the hells are you talking about?" Irena ground out after the pain seemed to subside. It wasn't as long as the last one and didn't seem to hurt her as much, thank the gods.

"What you are experiencing now is false labor. Your body is preparing to birth this child but isn't quite ready yet. Think of it as a trial run. You still aren't dilated, so you've got a while yet." The woman rose and collected her things, putting all her tools back in her bag. Dimitri hadn't even seen her get them out. "I'll have the kitchen send up some lavender tea to help you relax. I recommend you stay off your feet for the next day or so. Give your body a chance to recuperate. Have small meals, more frequently. I'll come back to check on you this evening." With that, the midwife picked up her bag and departed with the healer quick on her heels, closing the door behind them and leaving the three of them in a state of confusion.

"False labor?" Irena exhaled slowly. "If that was what fake labor feels like, I'm not sure I'll survive the real thing."

It was a bad joke, Dimitri knew that, but it didn't stop the ice from flooding his veins at the thought of losing her.

"Shut your damn mouth, woman," Tameer snapped, but

there was no bite to his words, only an edge of anxiety. He moved to stand, but Irena's body stiffened once more and she held onto both of their hands as though her life depended on it.

The contraction was over just as quickly, leaving his goddess looking drained, but less pale than when he'd first entered the room. Shifting slightly, he settled onto the floor at her side, never once lessening his grip on her hand. If she noticed his reticence to release her, she didn't react.

Nicolette slipped into the room, placing the water pitcher on the low table beside the chaise, and laying the cool cloth across the queen's pallid brow. Tameer retrieved a glass from the drink cart under the window across the small sitting room and filled it with water, gently handing it to Irena.

"I feel like such a fool," she said after taking a few deep drags of the water. Tameer refilled the glass and Dimitri squeezed her hand softly.

"You're not a fool, love." He offered her a warm smile. "We're all figuring this out. You were already handling it better than I was." He lifted one arm to reveal the sweat soaking through the fabric of his tunic. "I practically broke my own legs entering the room," he added with a chuckle.

"Yes, that was quite the dramatic entrance," Tameer teased. He retrieved two more glasses, filling these with ice and whisky before passing one to Dimitri.

Irena set her cup down and buried her head in her hands. "I don't think I can do this." Her words were partially smothered by her hands, but Dimitri heard her loud and clear.

Setting his own glass aside, he gently pulled her hands away, drawing her eyes up to meet his. "You are the strongest, most capable woman I've ever met. I don't believe there's anything you can't do. Including,"—he looked pointedly at Nicolette—"ousting that son of a bitch Gustave."

"Now?" Nicolette asked, a hint of incredulity in her voice.

"Why not? It seems our beloved queen could use a good distraction and it will definitely lift her spirits. Especially since she's been restricted to bed rest."

"What?" Irena protested. "I most certainly have not been! I'm the queen. I can't be confined to a bed for any length of time."

Dimitri raised an eyebrow in challenge. "Did you not hear your midwife? Rest. Relax. Stay *off* your feet. Let us take care of you for a while, love."

It was the second time he'd dropped the pet name in a matter of minutes, but he noted that she didn't seem bothered by it. In fact, she seemed to almost glow at his use of the word. Begrudgingly, she sighed and accepted defeat. Dimitri admired her spirit and the wisdom she exercised in knowing when she was beaten.

"Now, as to your distraction." Dimitri grinned broadly. "Nicolette and I have found a potential solution to your problem with Gustave."

"Oh, you've hired Leah, have you? I can't say I haven't thought about it, but I don't think it's the best option." Irena sat back on the lounge, adjusting her skirts and completely missing the look of confusion that Dimitri shared with Nicolette.

Tameer didn't miss it though. He cackled at their expressions and took a sip of his whisky. "You met Leah, Dimitri. Remember? She's the one who almost got you decapitated while flirting with you for information."

Right, the pink-haired baker. "I don't think he would have decapitated me..." Although the mountain of a man had had murder in his eyes for a few seconds.

Tameer's grin morphed into that of a fox. "Of course not, dear. Whatever you say."

"What does the baker have to do with anything?"

Irena looked up at him then, studying his face and realizing that he truly had no idea what she was talking about. "She's an assassin. You didn't know?"

Dimitri suddenly found it very hard to sit still. He stood abruptly and began pacing the room. "What? You're telling me that I was kidnapped and interrogated by an *assassin*? What the fuck? She said she was your friend! You're *friends* with a murderer?"

Irena patted the chaise beside her, inviting him to sit with her. Dimitri hesitated for only a moment before joining her. When he was settled, she cautiously took his hand—as though she wasn't sure she should—and explained. "Leah is my sister, for all intents and purposes. She's the one who saved me when I was a child and she's one of the few people in this world that I trust implicitly." Tameer cleared his throat at that. "I said one of the *few*. You're on that short list too, you needy ass."

Tameer saluted her with his whisky glass. "Good. I can't let

Leah think she's got something over me. I'll never hear the end of it."

Rolling her eyes, Irena turned her focus back to Dimitri. "I'm sorry they kidnapped you. That was *not* what I asked. I just wanted them to talk to you and make sure you were a decent guy before inviting you into this little charade." She waved her hand between the two of them.

A sly grin slipped across Dimitri's face as he asked, "I take it I passed?"

"With flying colors," Tameer said, refilling both of their whisky glasses, despite Dimitri having barely taken a sip. Tameer offered the decanter to Nicolette and Dimitri realized—too late—that they were openly discussing assassins, murders, and secret arrangements in front of the woman.

Irena followed his gaze and smiled. "Don't worry, love," she said, using his own word and filling his chest with a blooming warmth. "Nicolette is on my list as well. I wouldn't have survived my marriage without her." She reached out and took the handmaiden's hand, squeezing it gently, a look of love and unimpeachable trust on the queen's face.

Nicolette's face darkened to a soft blush as she returned the queen's smile.

"Now," Irena said, "if you haven't contracted my sister to kill my son-of-a-bitch advisors, what have you planned?"

SIXTEEN

Who knew royal advisors signed codes of conduct upon their induction into office? Irena sure as hells didn't. She understood now why Gustave and his predecessors had secreted away all the legal books behind armed guards. She'd never been more excited for her morning meeting. The thick legal book sat open before her, calmly awaiting the arrival of her soon-to-be-fired advisors.

Irena had decided to give the younger men an opportunity to reform their arrogant practices, but Gustave was out. She was practically vibrating with anticipation.

"You're in a good mood this morning, love." Dimitri entered the room with Tameer close behind him. Those two had become rather close over the last few days. They seemed to have thoroughly bonded over forcing her to stay in bed or on the lounge. It was equal parts sweet and infuriating.

Irena let a coy grin grace her face but didn't say a word as the rest of her council filtered in behind them. Once everyone was settled in their usual seats, with Dimitri standing behind her right shoulder and Tam a couple of steps behind him, Irena made a show of placing the tome on the table and flipping it open to the page she had previously marked.

Without introduction or context, she began to read. "The code of conduct for all royal advisors is as follows: One. Loyalty to the Crown. All advisors must put the betterment of Mistfall and her Royal family above all else. Advisors will serve with honor and courage, promoting the affluence of the country, as a whole. Two. Justice and Fairness. Advisors shall uphold justice, protecting the innocent and weak from oppression and unfair treatment under the law. Three. Truth and Integrity." At this, she paused, locking eyes with Gustave and glorying in the vibrant shade of rage-red that colored his puckered face. She'd memorized this part specifically so that she might look him in the eye as she said it. Irena wanted to see his face as she tore him down. "Advisors shall speak the truth at all times, maintaining their integrity above all else. They shall reject all manor of deceit and betrayal, honoring their devotion to Mistfall first and foremost, then their loyalty to the royal family."

She left the page open and sat back in her chair. Irena wasn't quite finished, but she wanted to give Gustave the opportunity to dig himself an even deeper hole.

The man's face seemed frozen in a state of unadulterated hate. He didn't dare speak though, so she sat forward. "The passage goes on. There are actually quite a few things on this list meant to keep you all honest and loyal. Surprisingly, I don't see a single face before me that hasn't violated this code in one way or another."

Tense silence descended on the room, but none of the men attempted to look at her. Their guilty eyes stayed fixated on the oak table in front of them.

"According to this, the penalty for violating even one of these rules is steep. Revocation of privileges, including forfeiting your rooms in the royal residence. Not to mention fines, public shame, and then there's the section on physical punishment." Irena cringed remembering the specific and descriptive ways advisors could be penalized. It was gruesome. "I don't want to have to take things that far."

"What is it you intend then, Your Majesty?" Gustave's voice was harsh, tight with fury while he tried to maintain his composure.

Irena gave him her most winning smile, goading him just a bit more. She was finally enjoying her time in this damned room and she wasn't about to let that feeling go. "I intend to give my council of advisors an opportunity to live up to the oath each and every one of you took upon accepting this position." She made a point to make eye contact with each man in turn, ensuring that they understood exactly what she was offering them. When her eyes turned back to Gustave, though, a wicked gleam met her. She knew he wouldn't be willing to take her offer, but Irena had argued with Dimitri and Tam about it the night before. She had to give him a chance. If for no other reason than to appear fair and generous to the rest of her council. She'd known from the start that Gustave would never back down.

"If you are willing to amend your practices," she continued, addressing the rest of the men. "Then we can consider this a clean slate. A fresh start. We will be hosting a Gathering at the end of the week, in which you will each take a knee and swear your oath to me and my child, reaffirming your commitment to Mistfall and her citizens."

Gustave scoffed. "And if we refuse your terms?"

"As I've previously stated, there are very clear penalties for violating your oaths to Mistfall and the royal family." Irena kept her voice calm and even. The other men were glancing around the room, silently debating her offer. She knew they'd accept her terms, though. These men had been advisors their whole lives. Many of them inherited their positions from their fathers, and their fathers before them. Irena fully intended to demolish this system of nepotism, but that would have to wait. For now.

Gustave huffed once more, then looked around the table. Irena hadn't thought it possible, but seeing his comrades taking her offer seriously, his face turned even more red. "You can't be considering this," he snapped at them. "She's not even the true queen. Just some harlot the king impregnated." He glowered at her, reaching into his vestments with an air of violence in his gaze.

Before he could move another inch, the blade of Dimitri's short sword was resting at the fool man's throat. Gustave froze in place as Dimitri pressed up gently, forcing Gustave to stand or have his throat speared through. "You will address your queen with the respect she deserves or I will have your tongue."

Eyes wide, Gustave nodded as subtly as he could, pulling his hand back out from within his robes and placing both palms down on the table. Dimitri kept his sword in place, looking at Irena for direction. She gave him a curt nod and he withdrew the weapon. Sliding it soundlessly back into the scabbard at his waist, he resumed his stance at her right.

Gods, that was unreasonably hot. She took a slow deep breath. Irena was a strong, independent woman, but seeing Dimitri instantly come to her aid, defending her honor, and then waiting for her permission to stand down was easily the most attractive thing he could have done. She fought the urge to fan herself.

Swallowing, she got back on task. "If you choose to take this offer, I expect you to be at the Gathering, ready and eager to swear fealty to me. If you choose not to, I expect you to vacate Ravendale before the Gathering begins. Those left who have not sworn their loyalty to me will be imprisoned."

It might have been harsh, but Irena was sick of being dismissed like a child and watching them drive Mistfall into the ground. She was their fucking queen. She was the authority in the room and they would either respect that or get the fuck out. Frankly, Irena didn't much care which way they chose.

"I look forward to your decisions," she said, effectively ending the meeting. The men rose awkwardly and began shuffling toward the door. Gustave, however, was still standing, hands on the table and hatred in his eyes. He wouldn't go quietly. No, he was far too stubborn and drunk with ill-gotten power. "Gustave," she addressed him coolly. "I would like your decision now. The rest of you may take the rest of the week," she added to her other advisors. "But Gustave, I need your answer now."

The man had the audacity to look smug. As though her calling him out was a mark of honor. Straightening himself, he clasped his hands before himself and gave her his most patronizing smile. "With all due respect, Your Majesty," he began, his words dripped with sarcasm. "I have no interest in being a lap dog for a childish whore like yourself."

Dimitri was on him in a heartbeat. Grabbing the arrogant old man by his collar and pulling him against Dimitri's own body, putting a dagger to Gustave's throat from behind. It was such a smooth and flawless series of movements that Irena didn't think Gustave could have defended himself at all. Dimitri moved almost as efficiently as Leah.

Irena kept her face blank, *tsk*ing Gustave's words as much as his behavior. "I was afraid you'd say something like that." She stood from her seat at the head of the table. "Guards!"

In an instant, four armed soldiers rushed into the room. Pushing passed the advisors who'd been rendered immobile as they watched the scene unfold before them. Dimitri roughly handed Gustave over to the guards, who bound his wrists and escorted him from the room. Irena had already asked them to have a cell made up for her head advisor.

King Odker had kept the prison cells dark, dank, and barren. Irena refused to treat anyone with such inhumanity, so she'd had the cells cleaned and was working to have barred windows installed in each one. For now, there were plenty of torches illuminating the whole prison, fresh straw was being brought in each week to replace the soiled flooring in the cells, and each prisoner was ensured three meals a day along with fresh, *clean* water.

Truthfully, it was better than Gustave deserved, but after seeing the place Ash had been locked away in, Irena knew she needed to reform the whole system.

Once Gustave was gone, the door closed behind him with a small click. The other advisors shared a nervous look, then quickly exited the room. Irena was confident they'd all be at the Gathering.

Dimitri and Tameer escorted Irena back to her rooms. Nicolette was already waiting for her when they arrived. Almost immediately, Irena yanked the crown from her head and handed it to her handmaiden. Dimitri understood how uncomfortable the royal headgear could be, but it was a little shocking to see just how quickly she wanted it removed from her person.

It wasn't an unattractive piece, to be sure, but the crown definitely wasn't what Dimitri would have picked. It was large, heavy, and overly adorned with an absurd amount of gemstones. It gave off a vibe of trying way too hard to show off one's wealth. Of course, he'd never say that to Irena. He did wonder if she'd actually gotten to pick out her crown or if she'd simply been given the crown of the previous queen.

In Westera, new royals are expected to sit with the royal

jeweler and design their own, unique crown. Looking around Irena's sitting room, Dimitri wondered if any of it was hers or if she'd inherited it all from the queen before her.

Tameer was already at the drinks cart when Dimitri took Irena's arm and guided—or rather, gently forced—her to recline on the chaise. He took a seat at the far end and lifted her feet into his lap. Carefully removing her gem-encrusted low heels, he set them aside and slowly massaged her swollen feet.

Irena let out the most delicious groan as she laid her head back and closed her eyes.

Tameer watched them for a moment, chuckling, and Dimitri fully expected him to make some smart-ass remark. Instead, he shook his head and poured himself and Dimitri each a glass of whisky. Nicolette brought in a steaming teapot and poured Irena a cup of herbal tea with a spoonful of honey.

"How did it go?" Nicolette asked as she set the teacup on the low table beside Irena.

Opening her eyes slowly, a broad grin spread across her face. "It went even better than I'd expected. I imagine they'll all be eager to swear loyalty to me at the Gathering."

"And Gustave?"

"Prison. That bastard had the nerve to insult our beautiful queen to her face and likely had a weapon. He looked poised to kill her." Dimitri accepted the drink from Tameer, throwing it back and placing the empty glass on the table. "The guards hauled his ass out of there."

"It was glorious." Irena beamed.

Dimitri watched her with pride. She'd been astounding in

that meeting. Cool, calm, and collected as she delivered her ultimatum. It was one of the sexiest things he'd ever seen. He pressed a knuckle into the ball of her foot, eliciting a moan that should have made him blush. Instead, it drove him wild as he repeated the motion. He watched her eyes flutter close and her mouth part ever so slightly. Gods, what he wouldn't give to kiss those lips once more.

Tameer cleared his throat, forcing Dimitri's mind back to the present. "I think we should let you two have a moment to celebrate this win." Tameer hooked his arm through Nicolette's. "What say you and I go find a decent bottle of wine and some dessert?"

Nicolette glanced at Irena for only a moment before nodding and letting Tameer lead her from the room.

Dimitri and Irena sat in companionable silence for a while, as he continued to massage her feet and she seemed to drift in and out of sleep.

"Your tea has gone cold," Dimitri said softly, rousing her from a light nap. "Would you like me to put the kettle back on?"

Irena blinked for a moment but shook her head. "No, thank you. Can we just stay here for a while longer? I'm not ready to get back to the real world just yet. I just want to be here in this moment with you."

Dimitri smiled down at her, feeling the exact same way. He nodded, shifting her feet in his lap.

"Would you..." she began but trailed off. She seemed almost nervous now that they were alone together.

"Whatever it is, I'd venture my answer will be yes." Dimitri offered with a warm smile.

She returned his smile, shifting her body and creating space beside herself. "Would you like to lay with me?"

Heat rushed his body, racing from his extremities and collecting in his groin. *Shit. Did she have to sound so sultry when asking such a question?*

She must have noticed his reaction because she quickly amended her question. "I mean, would you like to lie down beside me and take a little nap? Gods, I'm sorry." She blushed furiously. "I should really think before I talk."

"I don't know. The first question was quite an intriguing invitation." He winked making her blush deepen. Then he crawled up beside her, resting his head on the back of the chaise lounge and opening his arms to offer himself as a pillow for her head. When she accepted, he thought he might float away.

Irena curled into him, fitting perfectly in the crook of his arm as her head lay on his chest. Dimitri's heart was racing and he knew she could feel it.

"Oh!" she exclaimed softly.

Dimitri immediately moved to pull away, thinking he'd hurt her somehow, but she caught him with a simple hand on his chest.

"Do you want to feel the baby? I think they might be trying to dance in there." She smiled down at her protruding belly. Dimitri nodded into her hair and she took his hand. Placing it on the top of her stomach, she held it there for several moments. Dimitri was about to give up when he felt the sudden pressure of something pushing up, into his hand.

"Holy mother," he whispered. He'd felt babies squirming in his sister-in-law's belly once or twice, but to feel this child growing and stretching in the woman he loved? It was an entirely different experience.

"Yep," she said with a grin. "There's a real person in there. Weird, right?"

Dimitri chuckled, pushing back on her belly ever-so-slightly, as though he could play with the child through her body. To his surprise, the child responded with an answering kick. "Weird, maybe. Astonishing and amazing, definitely."

They drifted off to sleep cuddled together on the chaise, their fingers intertwined atop her belly as the baby danced within her.

SEVENTEEN

I rena woke to a sharp pain in her back and the feeling of something warm and wet leaking down her legs. Jolting up, she nearly knocked Dimitri off the lounge in her effort to get to her bathroom.

"What's happened?" Anxiety flooded Dimitri's words. "Are you ok?"

She didn't waste energy answering though, Irena was a hells-bent on getting to the bathroom, certain she'd just peed in her sleep and utterly mortified.

"Irena!" Dimitri called after her, panic lacing his voice.

"It's fine!" she called back, but she didn't manage any other words. Her voice—hells, her brain—cut off as a wave of pain unlike anything she'd ever experienced washed over her body. She clutched the wall and cried out as the agony passed through her.

Dimitri was by her side in an instant, grasping her arms and supporting her weight before she could crash to the floor.

"Talk to me. Please. What do you need?"

Through gritted teeth, she said, "Midwife." It was all she could get out as she forced herself to take deep breaths.

The baby was coming.

Dimitri had never felt more useless in his life. He yelled for the guards to fetch the midwife and held Irena until they returned with the midwife, healer, Tameer, and Nicolette. He'd carried her to the bathroom after Nicolette had finished filling the copper tub with warm water. He'd supported her weight as best he could as the healer and handmaiden helped Irena out of her many layers of clothing. When she was down to just her shift, he'd been the one to place her in the tub.

Through it all, Irena had done her best to focus on taking deep breaths. Dimitri took dramatic breaths with her, in solidarity maybe. Or just in an attempt to quell his own anxiety.

She moaned and swayed in the tub as Nicolette poured water over her stomach constantly. Dimitri watched in wonder as the muscles of her belly contracted, hardening like a rock as she groaned through the contractions. He held her hands when she let him and pulled her hair back from her sweat-glistening face when her grip became bone-crushingly painful. He wished, more than anything, that he could take her pain away, or take it for her. He hated seeing the agony awash on her face.

"Not much longer now," the midwife said with a smile. "You're fully dilated. This little one will be out before the sun sets."

"Thank the gods," Irena groaned.

Another contraction hit her and she ground her teeth to keep from shouting. Dimitri was in awe of her. Even in this state of emotional and physical distress, she was the most beautiful and amazing creature he'd ever seen.

"Keep breathing, Your Majesty." The midwife massaged the base of Irena's spine as Nicolette poured yet another pitcher of warm water over her stomach.

Grunting through the contraction, she squeezed her eyes closed and tried to steady her breath. "I... I think I might need to push." Irena's eyes flew open, panic dancing in her eyes.

"That's perfect, Your Majesty. With the next contraction, lean back and bear down. You'll get to see your baby soon." The cheer in the midwife's voice didn't touch the fear on Irena's face.

"I can't! I can't do this! I can't push a human out of my body!" Her breath was coming in short, rapid rushes. "I can't be a *mom*. I never had a parent. I have no idea what I'm doing!" Tears lined her lashes as another contraction took over. "No!" she cried out in pain and fear.

Dimitri shifted, putting his face directly in front of hers. "Irena. Irena, breath. Look at me." It took a moment, but her eyes finally met his. "You are a goddess. A magical, fierce goddess of power and female divinity. You *can* do this." He took her face in his hands, thumbs wiping away the tears that streaked down her cheeks. "You are the most amazing person I've ever met. This child is lucky to have you."

Irena studied him, eyes bouncing around his face as though looking for any sign of deceit. All she would find was love. Flowing out of him in unprecedented waves. She was his goddess and, if she let him, he'd spend the rest of his life convincing her of that fact.

"Are you ready?" he asked her quietly. She watched him a moment longer, then nodded.

"Your Majesty, if you'd like, your betrothed could join you in the tub. Most husbands choose not to be in the room for this part, but if you'd both like, Prince Dimitri, you could settle in behind Queen Irena and help support her while she pushes." The midwife moved from behind Irena to the other side of the tub, between the queen's legs, preparing to catch the child.

Dimitri looked askance at Irena. He was more than willing, but he didn't want to insert himself into her life more than she wanted. She nodded her consent without hesitation.

Dimitri shucked his boots, weapons, and belt faster than ever before and carefully climbed into the tub, sliding in behind Irena. She leaned back into him as soon as he was settled, another contraction quickly taking hold of her.

"We're going to push now. Deep breath and bear down as hard as you can."

Irena grasped Dimitri's hands and she clenched her teeth and pushed.

Gods, she was amazing. Over the next several contractions, she pushed through the pain and worked to birth the next royal of Mistfall.

"I can feel the head!" the midwife announced. "One more

good push and we should have a baby, Your Majesty."

Irena lay back, resting her head on Dimitri's chest as she tried to steady her breathing. Dimitri couldn't even imagine how exhausted she was. The sun was slowly disappearing behind the treeline out the bathroom windows. She'd been at this for hours.

"You've got this, love," he whispered, pressing a kiss to her temple. "Just a bit longer and you'll be holding that precious babe in your arms."

Nodding at his encouragement, Irena lifted her head, took a deep breath, and as the contraction started, she pushed with all the energy she could muster.

"Light hair," the midwife cheered. "Shoulders, arms... ah!" With the smooth movements denoting her decades of experience, the midwife coaxed Irena's child out and lifted the babe from the water. Grinning proudly, she offered the newborn to Irena. "Congratulations, Your Majesty. You have a son."

EIGHTEEN

A son. She had a son. Irena would never have to deal with her advisors undercutting her authority again. She was free to rule as she saw fit until her beloved little boy came of age. Irena cuddled her newborn close, smelling the sweet, magical scent that was uniquely his.

Once she'd been able to move, Dimitri had helped her to the shower and held her son while Nicolette helped clean her off and change her into a clean, breastfeeding-friendly shift. The healer had checked over her son as she lay in bed beside him, deeming him in perfect health and then the midwife and healer had departed. They assured her that they would be close by and come back to check them both in a few hours. Until then, she was instructed to rest and get as much sleep as possible.

Tameer beamed over his new nephew, watching the healer like a hawk while she inspected the babe, then hovering close while Irena learned to guide her son for the best latch while feeding. He was an excellent nursemaid and took careful notes while the midwife was there. Literal notes. He had a stack of papers in hand as the midwife gave Irena instructions and tips to ensure her son was getting all the nutrients her body could provide. It was adorable. At first.

After the third time Irena swatted his hand away as he tried to "help" adjust her son's head while nursing, she finally snapped. "Tam, darlin', why don't you head to the raven tower and send a message to Leah? She'll be pissed if she finds out we went through the whole night without telling her about this little man's arrival."

"You're just trying to get rid of me," Tam grumbled, but the smirk on his face took any sting from his words.

"Yes. Yes, I am. I don't need your hands all over my boobs, ok? Is that really so weird for you? Brothers aren't supposed to help their sisters *breastfeed*. It's creepy."

"What? It's not creepy. It's just skin! Skin I have zero interest in, aside from making sure my perfect little nephew is getting the most from it."

Irena raised an incredulous eyebrow at her brother. "Go," she said with finality. "And don't come back until after breakfast. I'm exhausted. I need sleep."

Tameer threw a nod over his shoulder. "What about him? Want me to take him with me?"

Dimitri was lounging in an armchair by the window, attempting to look casual while reading a book, but Irena had noticed he hadn't turned a single page in nearly an hour. He could have left any time, but he'd stayed. Hells, he'd climbed into that tub with her and endured her bruising grip to help bring her son into the world.

Irena glanced from her betrothed to the tiny bundle of blond hair and soft skin nuzzling her swollen breast. She'd been certain that labor would be the end of her. Irena remembered the pure, unadulterated pain, but only a few hours later, the memory was already turning fuzzy. Dimitri had been there for her. More than he needed to and likely more than any other man would have for a child that wasn't even his.

"He can stay, if he'd like." She spoke to Tameer, but her eyes were fixed on Dimitri's face, trying to read his reaction to her words. Did he want to stay or was he just trying to be polite in sticking around? Maybe he was only staying because the birth of a son meant she no longer needed their engagement and he was concerned for his own future.

Dimitri sat up, closing his book and rising from his chair. "I can leave, if you'd like to get some rest. I don't want to invade your space."

Irena smiled up at him. "I wouldn't mind if you wanted to stay."

She wasn't ready to admit out loud that she wanted him to stay forever. That hadn't been their agreement in the first place and she didn't know where his mind was at anymore. Irena felt herself falling for him, perhaps since they met, but she didn't know how he felt and she didn't want to trap him. Besides, she'd just given birth. Her hormones were all over the place. Irena resolved to not make any life-changing decisions until her hormones returned to normal.

"I'm happy to stay if you want—" Dimitri began but

Tameer cut in.

"He's gonna stay. I'll send a raven. Leah will likely be here by breakfast. Ash is still *persona non grata* around here, so I imagine he'll stay in Vexia. Now that you're the undeniable queen, I'm sure you'll be able to fix that." Tameer grinned. "You know, whenever you're able to get up and walk without waddling like you spent twelve hours riding a horse."

Irena scoffed, grabbing a pillow and throwing it at her brother. "Shut your mouth! You push a human out of *your* body and then you can talk shit about how I'm walking."

Tameer skillfully caught the pillow, tossed it back onto her bed, and practically danced out of the room.

"Gods, he's such an ass." Irena smiled, shaking her head as her focus shifted back to her son. "I suppose you need a name, don't you?" As her son released his hold on her, she covered her breast back and lifted her son so their faces were level. Irena hadn't put much thought into naming her child. When she'd first found out she was pregnant, she'd been so focused on dealing with Odker and surviving their marriage that she hadn't had the mental capacity for much else. Then, once that monster was gone, she'd poured all of her energy into fighting her council to improve her country.

"In my country, we don't name the children right away." Dimitri sat on the edge of her bed. "For the first year or so, the child is nameless while we wait to see what their personality is. Are they loud and outgoing? Adventurous and carefree? Or are they more cautious and intentional? It's a way to let the child have some say in who they are from birth."

Irena lowered the babe to lay across her lap. "That is a lovely tradition. What does Dimitri mean?"

Dimitri chuckled, pivoting and bending his knee so that he could sit more firmly on her bed and face her. "It means a devotee of Demeter. She's one of our more prominent deities. Goddess of the harvest and fertility. The story is that I would often toddle off and play in the wheat fields outside the royal residence. My mother took that to mean I was devoting my time to the goddess and named me accordingly."

A small smile tugged at her lips as she pictured toddler Dimitri, with his wild curls, sneaking around in wheat fields. Chasing mice and birds around in the tall stalks. She turned her warm smile back on her son, now deeply asleep on her outstretched legs. "I think that is a beautiful tradition. We will wait and see who he is before naming him."

We. She hadn't meant anything by it as the word slipped from her lips, but the way Dimitri's face brightened as he sat a little straighter, Irena knew that she would do whatever she could to convince him to stay with her forever.

The next few days were a blur of feedings, diaper changes, sleep, and visits from the midwife. By the end of the week, Irena was certain she would never feel well-rested again.

Tameer and Nicolette had taken over the planning and organizing of the Gathering. As much as she wanted to cancel the whole thing and spend the next three weeks in bed, Irena dragged herself out of bed the morning of the event and forced herself to shower. Her son was napping soundly in his bassinet with Nicolette watching over him while she worked the knots from her hair.

He was still fast asleep when Irena came out of the bathing room, robe tied loosely around her waist and her hair bundled in a towel. Nicolette had pulled out one of Irena's favorite gowns for the Gathering. The fabric was a deep purple, so dark it was almost black, but when the light hit it, it shimmered with varying hues of purple. Silver lace trimmed the bodice, with silver ribbons criss-crossing down the back.

Nicolette brushed and styled Irena's sandy blond waves into an updo worthy of a queen, topping it off with her hideous crown.

Her son was just beginning to wake when a guard knocked at her door. "Prince Dimitri to see you, Your Majesty."

"Send him in." Irena pushed up from the stool at her vanity, retrieving her child as Dimitri entered carrying a green box tied with a large teal ribbon. Irena recognized the packaging as that of the town's most sought-after jeweler. Nicolette glanced at the box, her eyes subtly widening. She clearly recognized it as well. She gave Irena a warm smile and slipped from the room, leaving Irena alone with her son and her betrothed.

Dimitri crossed the room with the confidence and purpose of a man on a mission. He placed the package on a small end table and offered her his arm. She accepted it and he guided her to take a seat on the couch. With her babe snuggled against her, Dimitri smiled down at them both, standing before them with a question clearly on his mind.

"I have always felt adrift in my life." He began, his voice surprisingly calm even as she felt her own heart racing. "Floating from one thing to the next without any real purpose or goal. But that night, when we first kissed, something in me clicked into place. Irena, you are my true north. My guiding light. I don't want to live my life without you and this child. If you truly wish for me to go, then I will without question. But I needed you to know how I felt before you made your final decision."

Tears lined her lashes and it took several deep breaths before Irena was able to respond. "I couldn't have survived these last few weeks without you. More importantly, I don't wish to continue without you." Her son fussed a little in her arms, causing them both to chuckle and beam down at the young prince. "I can't imagine our lives without you in it, Dimitri. Please stay."

The wide, shining smile on Dimitri's face outshone the sun. Tears glided slowly down her cheeks as Irena stood and Dimitri pulled her and her child into his arms. Wrapping them snuggly together, Irena embraced her new life. Her new little family.

Dimitri pulled back a moment, placing a firm kiss on her forehead before grimacing at the awful tiara on her head. A watery laugh escaped her lips as she teased him. "What? You don't like my exquisite crown?"

Dimitri hesitated for a second, as though trying to determine if she were being serious. "It just doesn't seem like *you*. In Westera, newly appointed royals design their own headpieces. I realize that's not the custom here, but I took it upon myself to have one made for you. This one,"—he gestured to the monstrosity on her head—"is lovely, and obviously you should keep it if you truly like it, but I thought this one might suit your tastes a bit more." He released her, stepping back to retrieve the box. Handing him the child, Irena took the box and sat back down to open it.

Her fingers were shaking as she gently pulled the ribbon and lifted the lid to reveal the most stunning thing she'd ever seen. Polished to a high shine and practically seconding as a mirror, the black metal crown was delicately designed with a handful of purple sapphires sparkling from the tips of the limb-like branches. It was regal without being overpowering or cumbersome. Sparkling with the gentle authority she strove to project.

"It's perfect," she whispered on an exhale. Gingerly, she picked up that lightweight tiara and turned it from side to side, studying the intricate leaf detailing embossed into the metal. The gemstones were made to look like the buds of flowers on a vine atop her head.

Dimitri gently laid the baby back in his bassinet and returned to her. "May I?" She nodded and he removed the heavy gold crown from her head, setting it aside and taking her beautiful new crown from her still shaking hands. The smile on his face was one of pride and love. She never wanted to go a day without seeing that smile ever again. He settled the crown on her head, placing another kiss to her forehead and guiding her to the vanity mirror. Irena couldn't believe how perfectly the crown matched her dress. It was as though he'd slipped into her mind and saw who she truly was and what she loved.

"How did you know?" she asked softly, unable to tear her eyes away from her own reflection.

"I just wanted to make you smile, love." He stepped closer behind her, wrapping his arms around her and locking eyes with her reflection. "You deserve to be queen and feel comfortable and confident in your environment. Especially when it comes to your crown. It's a representation of you and your authority. Now, it truly represents *you*."

Irena pivoted in his arms, wrapping hers around his neck and holding his gaze. "Thank you," she said, though her words sounded small and weak, she knew he felt the weight of their sentiment. "For everything."

"I will always be here for you, my queen. Whatever you need, just say the word. I love you, Irena."

His hands on her body were the only thing in the world. Irena sighed, melting into him and pulling his lips down to meet hers. There was a gentle, banked heat in his kiss. Pressing up on her toes, Irena deepened their kiss, slipping her tongue into his mouth and teasing his with her own. The moan that escaped his throat vibrated within her. Dimitri stepped closer, slowly driving her back against the vanity. The sound of glass bottles knocking together as she bumped into the table barely even register as she gripped his hair, twisting it in her fingers. She wanted him. All of him. Right now. Forever.

The sounds of her baby's quiet fussing broke the spell they were under. Breathing hard, their lips separated as Dimitri pressed his forehead to hers. He chuckled as he pulled her close, wrapping his arms around her waist once more. "I suppose we'll have to wait until nap time to continue this."

Irena smirked and nodded. "We do have much to discuss." She tugged teasingly at the hair at the base of his neck, eliciting another delicious moan from him. "Although, I fear it's only fair to warn you that the midwife strictly forbade me from sex for at least six weeks. Apparently, it's standard practice for new mothers."

"Well, your body did go through quite a bit to bring your son into the world." Dimitri nodded in agreement.

"*Our* son," she corrected pulling back to look him in the eye. "I realize he's not yours by blood," she began, blushing and suddenly very concerned that she might have overstepped.

"If you'll have me, I'd be fucking *thrilled* to raise this child, and any others, with you, my love. Blood doesn't make someone family. Family are the people you choose to spend your life with, and if you'll have me, I'll spend the rest of my days building this family with you."

Nineteen

Dimitri had never been to a Gathering before. Irena explained that it was a tradition that started during the time of clans. Once a year or any time a new laird was named, the clan would gather to pledge fealty to the laird and celebrate the coming year's bounty.

"These days, it's more of a celebration and a way to honor the start of the harvest season, but it's the perfect time to assert my true status as queen and weed out those advisors who aim to undermine me."

Irena insisted on carrying the newborn prince, rather than passing him off to Nicolette or the nursemaid. Dimitri hadn't bothered arguing the point. Irena had carried that babe for more than nine months. If she wanted to continue to carry him, who was he to disagree? Instead, he followed exactly two steps behind her. Their betrothal was true and *real* now, but he was intent on making sure the citizens of Ravendale, and Mistfall as a whole, knew she was the one in charge. They were her people first, and she would be the one leading them. Dimitri saw himself in a more advisory capacity. Available to her, should she need guidance in navigating foreign policy or courtiers, but she knew the people of Mistfall far better than he ever could. She was the ruler they deserved and he'd make damn sure no one got in her way.

The sounds of a bard and his accompaniment echoed through the hallway, drawing them in like a siren's song. The Great Hall was filled with the laughter and chatter of slightly intoxicated courtiers as Irena paused at the royal entrance. The guards stood at attention, banging the butts of their spears on the ground twice, then turning and leading the way into the Great Hall. The second the guards crossed the threshold, the music stopped and the chatter instantly died down. The herald sounded his trumpet loudly, ensuring that anyone who had somehow missed the arrival of the royal party would be well informed.

"Her Majesty, Queen Irena, the Crown Prince, and Prince Dimitri." The herald's voice was clear and Dimitri couldn't help but smile at the warmth that bloomed in his chest at being announced with the woman he loved.

Irena crossed the room, climbing the steps of the dais with the grace and beauty of the goddess she was, the young prince still sound asleep in his mother's arms. Dimitri followed behind her, moving to stand at her right shoulder as she reached her throne.

"I'm so pleased to see so many happy faces here today. It is an honor and privilege to serve as your queen. I'm looking forward to guiding Mistfall into the next age of progress and prosperity. In keeping with the traditions of the Gatherings of old, I have instructed all of my advisors that they may choose to retire from their positions or swear their allegiance to myself and my son, the Crown Prince. Those who have chosen to stay should be in attendance today." Dimitri followed Irena's gaze as she studied the room. He spotted the faces of nearly every advisor. Gustave was gone, and it seemed a couple of the other, older advisors, had chosen to take retirement instead. Dimitri stifled an annoyed sigh. Of course, they'd rather retire than serve a woman who knows what she wants and won't back down.

Irena glanced over her shoulder, nodding to Dimitri. He was up first. Tameer had walked him through the ritual a dozen times the night before, ensuring that he wouldn't fuck it up. The wording was old and odd, but traditions often were.

Stepping forward, Dimitri walked down the steps of the dais, pivoted on his heel, and dropped to a knee before his beloved. He pulled a small, ceremonial dagger from the sheath at his waist and lifted it up in offering. "By the steel of this blade and the blood in my body, I swear undying fealty to you, my queen. Should I break this oath, bury this blade in my heart and damn me to the deepest pits of hells." He took the blade, piercing the tip of his thumb, and squeezed a few drops of blood into a copper bowl that rested atop a wooden podium. "With this offering, I seal my oath."

"Arise, my loyal subject. I accept your oath and your fealty." Irena beamed down at him, her eyes glowing with love and adoration. Dimitri stood, bowed, and rejoined her on the dais.

A line had formed behind him while he'd knelt and offered his oath. No sooner had he taken up his stance two steps behind Irena that the next man began swearing the very same oath. Each man offered his dagger, his oath, and his blood in turn. By the end of the ceremony, the small copper bowl was half filled and glistening with the deep crimson of fresh blood. As the last man stepped away, Tameer retrieved the bowl and came to kneel before Irena, lifting the bowl in supplication.

Irena had warned Dimitri that this was the only part she was truly dreading. Traditionally, the laird or new leader would pierce themselves, mixing their blood with the blood of their devotees, but she wasn't sure she could stab herself. Irena had confessed to him that the sight of blood tended to make her nauseous, to which Dimitri had confusingly pointed out that her body bled monthly, and shouldn't she be used to blood by now? He'd never seen a person blush so thoroughly.

"Perhaps," she'd said, "but it doesn't change the facts. I will need you by my side, in case I faint." Dimitri had, of course, readily agreed.

As Irena stood before her people now, though, she looked calm and at ease. Nicolette stepped up and took the baby from her as Dimitri offered her his dagger. Raising the blade over her head, she addressed the crowd. "As you have sworn loyalty to me, I now swear mine to you. As your queen, I will strive to bring peace and prosperity to each and every one of you. I will protect you and work tirelessly to improve your lives. You are my people and I am yours." Taking the dagger from

Dimitri, she mostly hid her grimace and turned the point on herself. Pressing the sharp blade into the meat of her thumb, Irena stifled a wince and squeezed a few drops of her blood into the copper bowl. "May the gods bless us all."

The crowds cheered as the bard struck up the music once more. Tameer gave Irena a proud grin and a clean, white cloth to wipe the blood from her thumb. "You did it, kiddo," he congratulated her. Tam looked like he wanted to pull Irena into a hug, but restrained himself. Hugging the queen wasn't exactly appropriate behavior.

"Thanks," she returned his smile and the cloth.

"I'm just gonna..." Tameer nodded to the copper bowl still in his hand. "Where does this even go? Do I dump it out the window? It's fucking gross."

"It's not gross," Irena chided, but her lip curled of its own volition. "All right, maybe it's a little gross. But you can't just throw it away. Tradition dictates it be made into an ink and the advisors will all use that ink to sign their new codes of conduct." She waved a servant over. "Xavier, would you please deliver this to the wordsmith." Taking the bowl, the man offered Irena a deep bow and slipped out of the Great Hall.

"Gods, your traditions are fucking gross." Tameer sneered as he stared after the servant.

Irena laughed. "They're *your* traditions too, you know. You're Mistfallian, too."

Tameer looked ready to argue, but Dimitri stepped forward. He wasn't going to let them bicker through her first Gathering as queen. "Your Majesty," he said, drawing her attention away from Tameer and his snark. "Would you like me to clean that blade for you, my love?"

Irena glanced at her hand. She'd clearly forgotten she still held his dagger. "Oh, gods! Yes, please. Here." She handed him the blade as though it were on fire.

Dimitri chuckled under his breath, taking the dagger and wiping the blood off the sharp steel before slipping the weapon back into its sheath. Irena reached for his hand as soon as the dagger was safely stowed away.

"Thank you," she said, squeezing his hand to emphasize her words. "I couldn't have done any of this without you."

Dimitri pulled her into a gentle embrace, hugging his betrothed for all to see. Decorum be damned. He whispered into her ear, "My love, there is nothing on this planet that you can't do. And I can't wait to watch you show these people how truly amazing and powerful you are."

The Gathering was perfect. Only a handful of drunken scuffles that her guards managed to quell without bloodshed. Irena and Dimitri had made their royal exit after a couple of hours. Once the crown prince became fussy and eager for his next meal. Irena had steadfastly refused a wet nurse. She was committed to caring for her child the way her own mother had never cared for her. Tameer had called her stubborn. Leah had said she admired Irena's determination but also said if she ever had kids, she'd hire all the help she could afford.

Irena wished her sister could have stayed longer, but Leah had only been able to spare a day. Being Vexia's premier baker and a—mostly—retired assassin took up a great deal of her time. Irena promised to have Ash's pardon pushed through in her first meeting with her newly devoted advisors. He'd done a public service in removing Odker from power. She would ensure that her council saw it as such.

"He's finally asleep," Dimitri said, his voice barely above a whisper as he gently closed the bedroom door and joined her on the sofa. "Gods, you'd think after such an exciting party, he'd pass right out."

"We probably only have an hour or so before he wakes to eat again." Irena leaned into Dimitri's side, curling up against him and resting her head on his shoulder.

Dimitri's arm reflexively wrapped around her as he laid his head on hers. "There are so many things I could do for you in an hour." His voice was husky, sultry, sending a shiver down her spine.

Irena nuzzled into him farther, inhaling deeply his scent of sandalwood and ocean breeze. She felt him yawn against her brow, triggering an answering yawn from her as well. "Maybe we should nap a bit first."

Dimitri nodded slowly. "Ok, but then, I'm going to make your toes curl with ecstasy." His words were thick with exhaustion causing Irena to smile against his warm chest.

"Whatever you say, love," she replied drowsily.

They were both asleep in seconds, not waking again until the Crown Prince demanded sustenance.

Six weeks had seemed like ages when the midwife had told Irena she'd have to abstain from all carnal activities. Dimitri was considerably more patient and accepting of the concept. It was infuriating.

For the first couple of weeks, Irena was exhausted and her body was still recovering from the experience of pushing a human from her womb. But by the end of the third week, she felt perfectly fine and was ready to "get back on the horse," as they say. Dimitri was kind, considerate, and so fucking hot. Especially when he fell asleep on the bed with her son on his chest. Irena had never been more attracted to another creature in her life.

Thankfully, she had enough duties to distract her from her frustrations. Mostly.

Between wielding her newfound power and authority—and finally being able to pardon Ash for murdering her abusive husband and start construction on the plumbing for her citizens—planning a wedding, recovering from giving birth, and adjusting to life with a newborn, Irena was asleep the instant her head hit the pillow. However, they'd finally figured out a routine with the babe that seemed to be working. He obviously wasn't sleeping through the night, but he would sleep for a solid three or four hours before waking for his next meal, which always came from Irena.

One of her advisors had casually suggested she get a wet nurse when she'd started breastfeeding her son in the middle of a council meeting one afternoon. She'd politely informed him that if he was uncomfortable with her using her body as it was biologically designed, he could get the fuck out. No one has made a comment since.

Still, it was draining for her body to still not feel like her *own*. She'd gone from nightly abuse to pregnant, and now her body's primary focus was providing sustenance for her son. It was equal parts thrilling and exhausting to know that she was the only one caring for her child in such a vital way.

By the end of the fifth week, Irena was going stir-crazy. She slept next to the most beautiful man she'd ever seen every night. She could touch him, feel the warmth of his skin against her body and the tickle of his breath in her hair as she fell asleep with her head on his chest each night. And yet, despite their closeness, she desperately wanted to feel *more* of him.

On the very last day of the sixth week, Irena stormed into the midwife's exam room and jumped eagerly only to the exam table.

"Please, for the love of all things sexy and that godsdamned man in my bed, *please* tell me we can finally consummate our relationship."

The midwife rose from her desk, chuckling under her breath as she made her way across the room to assess Irena's recovery. "I didn't realize this forced abstinence would be so challenging for you, Your Majesty." The woman barely concealed the grin that tugged at her lips.

Irena collapsed back onto the exam table, throwing her arms over her face. "Have you seen him? It's taken all of my self-control to keep my hands to myself."

The midwife nodded knowingly. "Let me just take a quick look." She raised Irena's skirts and performed her exam as quickly and painlessly as possible. Irena loved that about the woman. She was kind and efficient in everything she did. "Everything looks perfect! You've healed quite nicely, Your Majesty. I dare say, you might even be ready for another babe before the year is over."

Irena scoffed, sitting up and lowering her skirts once more. "With all due respect," she said with a smirk, "I have no desire to birth another human for at least a year. Probably longer. I just want to enjoy my body again. As the gods intended." With that, she hopped off the table, thanked the woman, and sauntered out of the room in search of her betrothed.

Six weeks had been torture. Dimitri had known it would be a challenge to share a bed with Irena and not be able to touch her, make her feel as magical and beautiful as she should. He hadn't expected it to be *so* fucking hard. Hells, he was hard all the time. Just looking at her across the dinner table, licking a crumb from the corner of her mouth, or hearing the sounds she made as she savored the bacon in her mashed potatoes. It had been the most challenging experience of his whole—granted, highly privileged—life.

Tonight was the night, though. He'd been counting down the days and had arranged for Tameer and Nicolette to keep the baby for the night. Those two had grown very close over the last few months and they were both amazing with the young prince.

Irena had gone off to see her midwife after their last set of meetings that afternoon. Dimitri had requested their dinner be served in the queen's chambers. While they weren't married yet, the wedding date was set in stone, invitations had been sent out, and honestly, he really didn't give a shit. Every atom in Dimitri's body screamed to be closer to Irena. As close as two humans could possibly be.

It was fucking time. Pun intended.

Dimitri was just finishing lighting the last of the candles in Irena's bathing room when he heard the door to her chambers close.

"Dimitri?" his beloved called out. "Are you in here?"

Trying to keep his cool, in case the midwife had given her less-than-ideal news, Dimitri exited the bathing room, closing the doors gently behind him. That would be a surprise for later, regardless of their physical activities. His bride-to-be deserved a night of pampering and he was determined to give it to her.

"Here, love. Everything ok?" He tried to keep his voice causal, but he could feel his heart racing at the sight of her flushed skin. She'd clearly run all the way here from the midwife.

Irena's eyes were ablaze as she ran to him. With all the grace of a cat who'd fallen off the pier, Dimitri scrambled to catch her as she jumped into his arms. Wrapping hers firmly around his neck, she pulled him into the most intoxicating kiss he'd ever known. Her tongue sought entry which he readily granted as he adjusted his grip on her soft body. Slipping his hands down her body, he grabbed hold of her thighs and lifted her to wrap her legs around his waist.

A groan escaped his lips as her body pressed against his already-hardening cock. Irena smiled into his mouth.

"The midwife says I'm free to resume normal activities." She ground her body into his at the last word, eliciting another, considerably louder, moan from Dimitri.

"Thank the gods," he muttered. Pivoting, he carried her to the bed, all but tossing her onto it as he promptly climbed on top of her.

Burying his face in her neck, he gently bit her ear lobe and whispered, "I want to hear you scream my name until you lose your voice and mind in pleasure."

He pulled back a moment, to see the fiery passion in her eyes that he knew was reflected in his own. Dimitri was certain he would never get his fill of this majestic woman.

But that wouldn't stop him from trying every chance he got.

Also by Mallory Wanless

The *turmio* trilogy:
Storm and Flame: Enchanted I
Blood and Destiny: Enchanted II
Reign and Ruin: Enchanted III

Enchanted Standalones:
Reclaiming the Frost: Enchanted IV

Vexia Standalone Novellas:
Of Poison and Passion
The Royal Gambit

Coming soon:
Enchanted V
Enchanted VI

 Mallory lives in Texas with her husband and their two young boys. She spends her days home-schooling and full-time parenting. Her nights, and any free time she manages to carve out during the day, are devoted to reading and writing.

If you enjoy this story, please be sure to leave a review on your favorite sites. Thank you so much!

www.ingramcontent.com/pod-product-compliance
Lightning Source LLC
Chambersburg PA
CBHW061544310726
48972CB00008B/2603